The Spoils of Troy

LINDSAY CLARKE

This book is produced from independently certified FSC™ paper to ensure responsible forest management.

For more information visit: www.harpercollins.co.uk/green

HarperCollinsPublishers

HarperCollins*Publishers* Ltd
1 London Bridge Street
London SE1 9GF

www.harpercollins.co.uk

First published as part of *The Return from Troy* by HarperCollins*Publishers* 2005
This paperback edition 2020

ISBN: 978-0-00-837108-1

Printed and bound in the UK by CPI Group (UK) Ltd, Croydon CR0 4YY

SC™ paper

ık/green

For Phoebe Clare

For Phoebe Clare

Contents

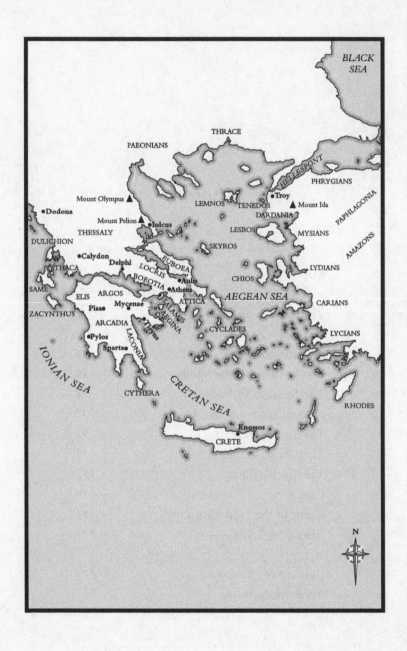

The Justice of the Gods

More than fifty years have passed since the fall of Troy. The world has turned harder since iron took the place of bronze. The age of heroes is over, the gods hold themselves apart, and my lord Odysseus has long since gone into the Land of Shades. It cannot now be long before I pass that way myself; but if honour is to survive among mortal men, then pledges must be kept, especially those between the living and the dead.

Thus I Phemius, bard of Ithaca, remain bound by the solemn pledge I made to Lord Odysseus on the evening when a few of us sat by the fire in his great hall discussing whether or not justice was to be found among the gods. I insisted that few traces of divine order were discernible in a world where a city as great as Troy could be reduced to ruin and yet so many of its conquerors were also doomed to terrible ends. What point was there in looking to the gods for justice when the deities could prove as fickle in their loyalties as the most treacherous of mortal men?

'That Blue-haired Poseidon should have wreaked his vengeance on the Argive host is unsurprising,' I declared. 'He had favoured the Trojans throughout the war. But Divine Athena had always been on our side, even in the darkest times. So how could she have forgotten her old enmity with Poseidon for long enough to help him destroy the Argive fleet? Such perfidy *would be appalling in a mortal ally. How then can it be excused in an immortal goddess?'*

Odysseus studied me in silence for a time. The expression on his face reminded me plainly enough that I might know all the stories by heart but I had never been at Troy myself and was speaking of matters that lay far outside my experience.

'Even a god's heart can be shaken by the sacking of a city,' he said. 'Even enemies can conspire when they find a common cause. As for myself, I believe that the gods see more deeply into time than we do, and what appears to us as mere caprice may eventually prove to be a critical moment in the dispensation of their justice.'

I saw him exchange a smile with his wife Penelope, who turned to me. 'Consider,' she said, 'what Grey-eyed Athena must have thought as she saw Locrian Aias trying to ravish Cassandra even in the sanctuary of her own shrine. Consider how the goddess must have felt when Agamemnon ordered her sacred effigy to be taken from Troy and carried off to Mycenae.'

'And those were not the only crimes and desecrations committed that night,' Odysseus added. 'If Divine Athena turned her face against us, it was with good cause. I can well imagine that she looked down through the smoke on the destruction of Troy and felt that she had seen enough of the ways of men to know that there could never be peace till they came to understand that the desolation they left behind them must always lie in wait for them elsewhere.'

It falls to me now to show how the truth of those words he spoke about Divine Athena was made manifest in the hard fates that awaited the Argive heroes after they celebrated their triumph at the fall of Troy.

The Fall

Odysseus stood in the painted chamber high inside the citadel of Troy, listening to the sound of Menelaus sobbing. Spattered in blood, the King of Sparta was sitting on a bed of blood with his head supported in his blood-stained hands. Helen cowered at his back, white-faced. The mutilated body of Deiphobus lay sprawled beside him. Though the streets outside rang loud with shouts and screaming, here beneath the rich tapestry of Ares and Aphrodite it felt as though time itself might have halted to hear Menelaus weep.

Even Helen, whose delinquent passion had precipitated all these years of suffering, had ceased to whimper. Having been so appalled by the sight of warm blood leaking across the bed that she might have screamed and been unable then to cease from screaming, she was now staring at her husband with a kind of wonder. For the first time in many weeks she was thinking about someone other than herself, and feelings that she had long thought petrified began to stir with an almost illicit tenderness. Was it possible then that, for all the offence she had given him, and all the anguish she had caused, this gentle-hearted man still loved her?

Afraid that she might break the spell that had so far spared her life, she raised a bare arm and stretched out her hand to comfort his quaking shoulder.

Instantly, as though that touch had seared like flame, Menelaus pulled away. He leapt to his feet and turned, lips quivering, to stare down at the woman lying beneath him. Unable to endure the naked vulnerability of her breasts, his gaze shifted away to where Deiphobus lay with his eyes open and blood still draining from the ragged stump of the wrist. Menelaus bared his teeth and uttered a low growl. Dismayed that he had been so visibly overcome by weakness, resolved to countermand all signs of it, he picked up his sword from where it had fallen to the floor and began to hack once more at the lifeless flesh.

Watching Helen cower across the bed, Odysseus knew he had seen enough. If, in his madness, Menelaus desired to murder the woman who had betrayed him, that was his business. Odysseus would not stay to witness it. Silently he turned away and passed through the door, leaving his friend to do as he wished with the dead body of his enemy and the terrified, living body of his wife.

As he stepped out into the night air, he caught a smell of burning drifting upwards from the lower city. From somewhere in the distance, beyond the walls, he made out the din of swords beating against shields: a host of Argive warriors were still climbing the ramp and roaring as they poured through the open gate. Hundreds – perhaps thousands – more were already inside the walls, taking command of the streets and extinguishing whatever resistance the bewildered citizens were managing to muster. The nearer sounds of screaming and shouting were hideous on his ears. Yet it would all be over soon, Odysseus thought as he crossed the courtyard of Helen's mansion; the Trojans would come to their senses and lay down their arms in surrender of their captured city. Even to the bravest and most fanatical among them, any other course of action must soon come to seem futile and insane. But he was worried by that smell of burning.

When he came out into the street he found the cobbles underfoot slippery with blood and he was forced to pick his way among the corpses. Here they were mostly top-knotted Thracian tribesmen who lay thrown over one another in lax postures, with slack jaws, like too many drunkards in the gutters. There was no sign of movement anywhere among them. From the top of the rise, beyond their silence, came the shouts of Argive soldiers and a terrible screaming.

Afterwards Odysseus would wonder how he could not have been prepared for what awaited him there. After all, he had sacked towns before. He had killed men and taken women into slavery. In the heat of battle he was as ruthless as the next man and had never lost much sleep over what he had done. It was the way of things. It had always been so and nothing would change it. Yet when he turned the corner and saw three Spartans laughing as they tugged at the legs of a white bearded-old man who was trying to climb over a wall, then thrust their spears through his nightshirt into his scrawny belly, he was not prepared. He was not prepared for the way, all along the street, doors had been broken down and the terrified, unarmed figures of men and boys were being driven from their homes at spear-point and cut down by the warriors waiting for them.

When Odysseus saw their sergeant swing his sword at the neck of a sobbing youth with such force that it almost severed the head, he grabbed the man by the shoulder, shouting, 'In the name of all the gods, what are you doing? These people aren't putting up any resistance.' But the sergeant merely shrugged and said, 'So what? They're Trojans, aren't they?' and turned away to pull the next cowering figure towards the sweep of his sword. Odysseus saw the naked man's throat splash open as he crumpled and fell. He looked up through a slaughter-house stench of blood and saw such deft butchery repeated again and again along the length of the street while women with their hands in their hair stood screaming as they watched. One of them threw herself over the body of her husband only to be dragged away while a burly axe-man finished him off.

Odysseus shouted out a demand to know who was in command here, but his voice was lost in the shrieking of the women and he received no answer. He pushed his way along the street, making for the square outside the temple of Athena, and saw Acamas, son of Theseus, who had ridden inside the wooden horse with him, holding a man by the hair as he twisted his sword in his guts. Hearing Odysseus shout out his name, Acamas looked up, smiled in recognition, let the man drop, and stepped back, wiping the sweat from his brow.

'It's going well,' he said as Odysseus came up to him.

'But none of these people are armed,' Odysseus shouted above the din. 'There was an agreement.' He took in the warrior's puzzled frown. 'We gave Antenor our word!' he shouted. 'We said we'd spare the lives of all those who surrendered.'

Acamas glanced away at where his men were working their way like dogged harvesters through a huddled crowd of Trojan men and boys trapped in a narrow corner of the street. 'That's not what I was told,' he said. 'We're under orders to kill the lot and that's what we're doing. It's the same all over the city.'

'That can't be right,' Odysseus protested. 'Where's Agamemnon?'

'Probably strutting through King Priam's palace by now. I haven't seen him.' Acamas wiped a bloody hand across his mouth. 'Come on,' he said, 'there's still a lot of work to do.' Then he turned away, lifting his sword.

In what should have been the most glorious hour of his life, Odysseus was seized by a numbing sense of dread. To fight in open combat across the windy plain of Troy had been one thing: this slaughter of defenceless men, stinking of piss and panic as they stumbled from their sleep into narrow alleys from which there could be no escape, was quite another. Yet the havoc in these streets had already run so far beyond control it was clear that any male Trojan, man or boy, would be lucky to survive the night.

In a fury of disgust, Odysseus turned to push his way through the throng, looking for Agamemnon. The smell of burning was stronger now and through a thickening gush of smoke a lurid flame-light glared out of the darkness of the lower city. If fire had broken out among the weaving halls with their bales of cloth, reels of yarn, and timber looms, then more people might be burnt to death or trampled in the scramble for safety than would fall to the sword. The dogs of the city barked and whined. Coarse laughter surrounded a frantic screaming where a man was being tormented somewhere. Women cried out as they were pulled from the sanctuary of holy altars and driven like geese along the streets. Children sobbed above the bodies of their fathers. And when Odysseus strode into the square before the temple of Athena he saw the immense moonlit form of the wooden horse, like a monstrous figment from a dream, looming in silence over the spectacle of a city in its death throes.

Sick with shame, he remembered how he had harangued the troops on the day when it looked as though they might refuse to follow Agamemnon when he called for a renewed assault on the city. That had been months ago but he remembered how he'd incited them with the thought of the women waiting to be raped inside these walls. How easily the words had sprung to his lips. How little thought he'd given to the price they would exact in human suffering. But now Odysseus stood in the shadow of the horse that had sprung from his imagination, watching men kill and die in helpless multitudes. In conceiving his clever stratagem to breach the unbreachable walls of Troy, he had released ten murderous years of rage and frustration into the streets of the city. Never had he seen so many people cut down like cattle in a hecatomb. Never before had he felt so entirely culpable. When he looked about him, there seemed no limits to the horror he had wrought.

Still shaking from having seen her husband's head lopped off by that monstrous boy Neoptolemus, Queen Hecuba was among the first of the women to be dragged beneath the open portico in the square. Her younger daughters, Laodice and Polyxena, were supporting her feeble frame while the women of the palace followed behind, wailing and tearing at their hair. Neither Cassandra nor Hector's widow, Andromache, were anywhere to be seen.

Not long ago, for a few brief hours, the Trojan Queen had lain beside her husband in a dream of unexpected peace. Now the world had turned into a phantasmagoria around her aged head and so intense was the feeling of nightmare, so violent the alteration in her circumstances, that she could no longer trust the evidence of her senses. It was impossible that Priam lay dead with his regal head severed from his body. It was impossible that these streets and squares, which only a few hours earlier had been filled with thankful prayers and jubilant with revelry, should now echo to the brutal shouts of foreign voices and the anguish of her frightened people. It was impossible that the bronze helmets and armour of the soldiers dragging her away were anything other than the figments of a dream. Yet she knew from their gaping eyes and mouths that her womenfolk were screaming round her and, after a time, Queen Hecuba came to understand that she too was keening out loud with all the strength of her lungs.

Lifted by the breeze from the burning buildings in the city below, smoke gusted across the square so that the staring head and arched neck of the wooden horse seemed to rise out of fog. The women were left coughing as they moaned. Spectral in the gloom, their faces blemished by the streaks of paint running from their eyes, they looked more like creatures thrown up from the underworld than the graceful ladies of royal Troy they had been only an hour earlier. Then they were screaming again as the armoured figure of the herald Talthybius strode out of the torch-lit smoke. He was clutching the slender, half-naked figure of Cassandra by the arm.

The girl's eyeballs had turned upwards and she was singing to herself, not for comfort but in a crazy kind of triumph. Hecuba recognized the words from the Hymn to Athena. As though unconscious of the terror around her, Cassandra was singing of how, when the armed goddess sprang with gleaming eyes from the head of Zeus, all the gods had been awe-struck and the earth itself had cried out and the seas had stood still.

Pushed out of the swirl of smoke into the throng of women, Cassandra too might have sprung in that eerie moment from some unnatural source. But the suave pragmatist Talthybius had his attention elsewhere. Seeing Hecuba shivering in the night air, he berated their guards for putting the health of these valuable captives at risk. He ordered one of them to raid the nearest house for throws and blankets before the women caught their death of cold. Then he turned to confront the Trojan Queen where she stood with the cloth of her gown hanging open to reveal her depleted breasts.

'Forgive me for not observing your plight earlier, madam. The guards should have shown greater courtesy. But I beg you to calm these women.' Talthybius raised both his staff and his voice to silence the captives. 'The High King himself has commanded that you be brought here to safety and kept under guard. No harm will come to any of you. You have my word on that.'

'No harm!' Hecuba's thin grey hair had come unbound. It was blowing about her face like rain in wind. 'You think it no harm to see our men struck down? You think it no harm to watch our city burn?'

'Such are the fortunes of war.' The herald glanced away from the accusation of her eyes. 'Your husband would have done well to think of this when he threw our terms for peace back in our teeth all those years ago.'

'Do not dare to speak of my husband, Argive. The gods will surely avenge what has been done to him.'

'Isn't it already clear that the gods have set their faces against Troy?' Talthybius sighed. 'Be wise and endure your fate with all the fortitude you can.'

Reaching out to take Cassandra into the fold of her arm, Hecuba said, 'The Queen of Troy has no need of Agamemnon's lackey to teach her how to grieve.'

'The Troy you ruled has gone for ever, madam,' the herald answered. 'You are Queen no longer. When this night's work is done, you and your kinswomen will be divided by lot among the

Argive captains. I pity your condition but things will go easier with you if you school yourself in humility.'

'Do as you like with me,' Hecuba defied him. 'My life ended when I saw Hector fall. It was only a ghost of me that watched my husband die. What remains here is less than that. Your captains will find no joy in it.'

Talthybius shrugged. 'It may be so. But I give Cassandra into your care. Be aware that my lord Agamemnon has already chosen her for his own.'

'To be at the beck and call of his Spartan queen?'

'To be the companion of his bed, madam.'

Hecuba looked up at him with flashing eyes. 'I would strangle her with my own hands first.'

But at that moment Cassandra reached her fingers up to her mother's face and held it close to her own. She was smiling the demented smile that Hecuba had long since learned to dread. 'You have not yet understood,' she whispered. 'This is what the goddess wants of me. I have seen her. I saw her in the moments when they sought to ravish me beneath her idol. Divine Athena came there to comfort me. She told me I would be married to this Argive king. She told me that we must light the torches and bring on the marriage dance, and go joyfully to the feast. So that is what we will do. And you too must dance, mother. You must dance with me. Come, weave your steps with mine. Let us rejoice together and cry out *evan! evoe!* And dance to Hymen and Lord Hymenaeus at the wedding feast,' – her voice dipped to a whisper that the herald could not hear – 'for Athena has promised me that this marriage will destroy the House of Atreus.'

And then, as Hecuba looked on in dismay, Cassandra broke free of her grasp and began to stamp her foot and clap her hands above her bare shoulder, crying out to the bewildered Trojan women to join her in the dance and honour the husband who would shortly share her marriage bed.

'Look to your daughter, madam,' Talthybius warned. 'I fear she is not in her right mind.' Then, commanding the guards to keep a watchful eye on both women, the herald left the square to go in search of his master.

Slowly the hours of that terrible night dragged past. The women trembled and wept together. As if drugged on her own ecstasy, Cassandra slept. Exhausted and distraught, her throat hoarse from wailing, her breasts bruised where she had pummelled them in her grief, Hecuba entered a trance of desolation in which it seemed that no more dreadful thing could happen than she had endured already. And then Hector's widow, Andromache, was brought through the gloom.

Hecuba did not see her at first because her eyes were fixed on the twelve year old warrior Neoptolemus, who strode ahead of Andromache wearing the golden armour that had once belonged to his father Achilles. The last time she had seen this ferocious youth he had been standing over Priam's body looking down in fascination as blood spurted from the severed arteries of the neck. Still accompanied by his band of Myrmidons, Neoptolemus was carrying his drawn sword but he had taken off his helmet so that for the first time Hecuba could see how immature his features were. Only a faint bloom of blond hair softened his cheeks, and the eyes that surveyed the captive women were curiously innocent of evil. They were like the eyes of a child excited by the games.

Unable to endure the sight of him, Hecuba glanced away and saw Andromache held in the grip of two Myrmidon warriors. It was obvious from her distracted eyes and the uncharacteristic droop of her statuesque body that they were there to support rather than restrain her. The women of Hector's house followed behind, weeping and moaning. Evidently hysterical with terror, the body-servant Clymene seemed scarcely able to catch her breath as she gripped and tore the tangles of her hair.

Neoptolemus gestured with his sword for the women in his train to be brought forward and herded with the others. But when

Hecuba held out trembling hands to receive Andromache into her arms she was appalled to see her daughter-in-law stare back at her without recognition through the eyes of a woman whose memory was gone.

Though Andromache said nothing Hecuba could hear her breath drawn in little panting gasps as though she was sipping at the air. Her cheeks and throat were lined with scratches where she had dragged her fingernails across the surface of the flesh. A bruise discoloured the skin around the orbit of her right eye, and there was such utter vacancy in the eyes themselves that Hecuba knew at once that this woman had already been made to endure the unendurable.

'Where is your son?' she forced herself to ask. 'Where is Astyanax?'

Andromache's eyeballs swivelled in panic as though at sudden loss. Then memory seared through her. Again, as though the scene were being played out before her for the first time, she saw Neoptolemus dragging Astyanax by the lobe of his ear across the upper room of her house. Again she saw the deft sweep with which the young warrior lifted her child above the parapet of the balcony. Again she released a protracted scream of refusal and denial, and again it was in vain. Neoptolemus opened his hands and Astyanax vanished, leaving only a brief, truncated cry on the night air.

Unable to stop herself, Andromache had run to the balcony and gazed down where the small body of her son lay twisted on the stones twenty feet below. A pool of blood oozed from his head like oil. In that moment she would have thrown herself from the parapet after him if Neoptolemus had not grabbed her by the arm and pulled her away. So she had stood with that gilded youth bending an arm at her back, screaming and screaming at the night.

But even the mind has its mercies and, for a time, Andromache had slipped beyond the reach of consciousness. When she was pulled back to her senses, she woke into an alien land of torchlight, noise and violent shadows. If she had been asked her own name she could not have recalled it. Still in that primitive state of near oblivion, she had been conducted through the streets of Troy until she was brought to the moment when Hecuba asked after Astyanax. At the sound of the name a whole universe of pain flashed into being again.

Wiping the back of his hand across his nose, Neoptolemus stepped forward to look more closely at the terrified group of women huddled beneath the portico. Wrapped in blankets now, their heads held low in the gloom, they were hard to distinguish from each other. He used the blade of his sword to edge one woman aside so that he could see the girl cowering behind her. 'The boy had no father,' he was muttering, 'and now the mother has no son. But I have a remedy for that.'

Hecuba reeled where she stood. She felt as though she was striding against a dark tide and making no progress. She had seen her firstborn son Hector slain before the walls of Troy. She had seen her second-born, Paris, lying on his deathbed pierced and half-blinded by the arrows that Philoctetes had loosed at him. Others of her sons had failed to return from the battlefield. She had seen one of the youngest, Capys, die that night, cut down trying to defend his father. Then Priam himself had been murdered under her bewildered gaze. Now her six year old grandson Astyanax, Hector's boy, who had been the only solace that remained to her in a world made unremittingly cruel by war, was also dead. Somewhere she could hear Neoptolemus saying, 'One of you must be Polyxena, daughter of King Priam. Come forth. The son of Achilles wishes to speak with you.' Had she not already been exhausted by atrocity, every atom of her being would have shouted out then in mutiny against the gods. As it was, this latest devastation had left the Trojan Queen reduced to the condition of a dumb animal helplessly awaiting the utter extinction of its kind.

And no one among the women moved.

'Come, Polyxena, what are you afraid of?' Neoptolemus cajoled. 'I understand that my father was fond of you. It's time that we met.'

Still there was no movement among the huddle of blankets.

From somewhere Hecuba found the strength to say, 'Haven't you brought evil enough on Priam's house?'

The boy merely smiled at her. 'We Argives didn't seek this war. Troy is burning in the fire that Paris lit. We're looking only for justice here. As for me, remember that this war took my father from me. He might still have been living at peace on Skyros with my mother if your son hadn't taken it into his head to meddle with another man's wife. Now tell me, where is your daughter, old woman?'

But at that moment the sound of Agamemnon's voice boomed from across the square, shouting out his name and demanding to know where his generals were. As Neoptolemus turned to answer, Odysseus stepped out of the shadow of a nearby building, holding his boar-tusk helmet in the crook of his arm. Immediately Agamemnon demanded to know where he had last seen Menelaus.

'I left him with Helen,' Odysseus answered. 'Deiphobus and his household are dead. The Spartan Guard have control of his mansion.'

'Has he killed the bitch?'

'I don't know. Not when I left.'

Detecting an unusual shakiness in the Ithacan's voice, Agamemnon looked at him more closely. 'What's the matter with you? Have you taken a wound?'

'Have you seen what's happening down there? Have you seen the blood in the streets? I gave them my word – I gave *our* word to Antenor and Aeneas that we would spare all the lives we could. But this . . .'

Brusquely Agamemnon interrupted him, 'Aeneas and his Dardanians have already gone free. Antenor is safe enough if he stays indoors. And I've got my mind on other things right now. Memnon's Ethiopians have broken out of their barracks. Diomedes and his men are having a hard time containing them.'

He would have turned away but Odysseus seized him by the shoulder and stopped him. 'Antenor only agreed to help us because I gave him the most solemn assurances. I gave them on your behalf with your authority. Now you have to get control of this or they're going to kill everybody. You have to do it now.' But then he caught the shiftiness in the High King's eyes. His heart jolted. 'Are you behind this bloodbath?' he demanded. 'Is this what you want?'

Agamemnon shrugged the hand from his shoulder and walked away to where Neoptolemus had abandoned his search for Polyxena and was now assembling his war-band for action.

'Move your Myrmidons down into the lower city,' Agamemnon ordered. 'If you look lively we should be able to trap Memnon's men between your force and Diomedes. I want it done quickly.'

The young warrior raised his sword in salute and, to a rattle of bronze armour, the Myrmidons jogged out of the square down a narrow street that would bring them out in the rear of the Ethiopians.

Agamemnon looked back with displeasure over the city he had conquered. 'We need to start fighting this fire before half the treasure of Troy is lost to it.'

He was speaking to himself but Odysseus had come up behind him, determined to get the truth from him. 'You intended this all along,' he said. And when no answer came, 'You never meant to hold on to Troy as we planned, did you? You were just making use of me to deceive Antenor and Aeneas.'

'I've no time for this,' Agamemnon scowled. He was about to walk away when he was snagged by a need to justify himself further. He looked back at Odysseus again. 'Your stratagem of the horse worked well, old friend. Troy is finished. Poets will still be singing of this victory a thousand years from now. And you'll be back home on Ithaca soon enough, a rich man, tumbling your wife on that great bed of yours.' He grinned through the smoke at the grim face that frowned back at him, white as wax, in the moonlight. 'Think of it, Odysseus. Just think of it. We are immortal, you and I. Whatever happens, our names are deathless now.'

And with that, Agamemnon, King of Men, summoned his bodyguard around him once more and advanced towards King Priam's palace.

All night long, not speaking, refusing to be touched, Menelaus prowled the bloody chamber where the bed had begun to stink like a butcher's stall. Helen crouched in a corner, stifling her whimpers. Sometimes, as the night wind gusted, smoke blew into the room, charring the air. After a time the oil-lamp that had been left burning on a tripod guttered out. Now the darkness was almost complete.

Menelaus went to the balcony once to look for the source of the fire and saw that the mansion was in no immediate danger. Beneath him, a tumult of screaming people ran along the street, looking back over their shoulders to where a company of spearmen advanced towards them rattling their shields. But he took almost as little interest in what he saw as did the many corpses already cluttering the gutters. He was remembering those moments in the bull-court at Knossos when he had first heard the news of Helen's defection – how the roaring of the crowd had dimmed in his ears so that it sounded like the distant throbbing of the sea; how time had wavered strangely, and he had been possessed by the feeling that nothing around him was quite real.

Now it was much the same, for he was as little moved by the sacking of this city as he had been by the antics of the dancers in the hot arena or by the sleek rage of the bull. All this din and terror amounted to nothing more than an incidental accompaniment to the unappeasable clamour of his grief.

Menelaus could no longer see what was to be done. He had come to Troy with a single clear purpose in mind. But Paris had escaped him, fleeing from their duel in the rain like the craven coward he was. And though he had fallen later to the arrows of Philoctetes, it was an end in which Menelaus could take no pleasure because it deprived him of the personal satisfaction he had sought. And then, when the sickening news came that

Deiphobus had taken Helen to his bed, Menelaus had found a new and still more violent focus for his hatred. Because of this further insult to his heart, he had driven on the Argive generals to fight when it looked, for a time, as if the two exhausted armies might settle for a negotiated peace. He had reminded them of the oath they had sworn to him in Sparta. He had made it clear that he would be satisfied by nothing less than the death of Deiphobus. So the war had gone on and now the war was won. Troy had been taken, as Helen had been taken, by stealth and treachery. Deiphobus was dead, and Menelaus had made sure that he had known in the moment of his death exactly who it was that killed him. But his body lay on the bed like the joints of horse-meat on which the princes of Argos had sworn to defend Menelaus's right to Helen, and his troubles were now over. Yet even as Menelaus had hacked at his body, severing the head and limbs and genitals with his sword, he had found no satisfaction in the act. His arms were sticky with the man's blood. His face was splashed with it. And almost as strong as the grief in the King of Sparta's heart was the wave of disgust that left him retching in the night.

And still Helen lived.

Already Menelaus knew that if he was going to kill her he should have done it when he first found her in bed beside Deiphobus. But he told himself that he had wanted her to see her lover die. He wanted her to know how terrible his vengeful fury was. He wanted her to see what she had done to him, to learn how she had turned his gentle heart into a murderous thing. So the moment in which he might have acted had passed. And still, as she crouched in the corner like a frightened animal, he could not bring himself to finish her.

Nor could he command anyone else to do the deed.

Menelaus walked back from the balcony into the room and stood leaning against the door. He was still holding his sword. With the back of his free hand he tried to wipe the flecks of vomit from his mouth only to realize that the hand itself was wet with blood.

What was to be done? What was to be done? All across the city his comrades exulted in their triumph. Agamemnon must already be sitting on Priam's throne. Young Neoptolemus would be taking bloody vengeance for his father's death. The others would be revelling in the slaughter, toasting each other in captured wine as the women fell into their hands, or stripping the sacked palaces and temples of their treasure. Only he on whose behalf this long war had been fought stood in the darkness, empty and wretched, rejoicing at nothing.

Though the pain of the memory was almost more than he could bear, he was remembering the days long ago, in another time, in another world, when he and his wife had played together with their little daughter Hermione in the sunlit garden of the citadel at Sparta. How could Helen have dreamed of turning her back on such happiness? What must he himself have lacked in manhood that she should have spurned the unquestioning, utterly trusting fidelity of his heart, for a mad act of passion that could only ever have ended in disaster such as this?

Never, in all the long years since Helen had left him, had Menelaus felt so utterly alone.

Odysseus stood alone in the lurid night, beating his brains with the knowledge that this catastrophe was of his making and that he had intended none of it. His plan had been clear enough. He had discussed it carefully with Agamemnon and secured his agreement. Odysseus had always maintained that the long-term gain must be greater if the victorious Argives exploited the trading strength of Troy's position rather than merely despoiling the city of its wealth. With this larger aim in mind he had pursued his secret negotiations with Antenor and Aeneas, and he had done so in good faith, certain that King Priam and Deiphobus would be more easily deceived by the stratagem of the wooden horse if the distrusted minister and the vacillating Dardanian prince were seen to suspect it. So the city would fall by stealth and need hardly be damaged in the taking. Crowned as a client king once Priam was dead, Antenor would owe his throne and his loyalty to Agamemnon. The presence of a strong garrison in the city would underwrite the alliance. And then, with Troy secured as an Argive fiefdom commanding trade with the Black Sea, the entire eastern seaboard must sooner or later fall under Agamemnon's control. Meanwhile, Odysseus would go home to Ithaca a wealthy man, having crowned the Lion of Mycenae as undisputed ruler of an Aegean empire.

It was more than a plan: it was a vision – a vision that would change the map of the known world for ever. Even as he had climbed the ladder into the wooden horse, Odysseus had been sure that Agamemnon understood the dream and shared it. But he had come out of Helen's mansion and stepped into a massacre.

The fire, he was prepared to concede, might have started by accident. But if, with the low cunning and purblind greed of a common soldier, the King of Men had already decided to opt for quick profit rather than the long-term benefits of a less certain vision then the logic became inexorable. To prevent Troy rising again and descending on Argos with the force of the avenging Furies, the destruction must be complete. The city must be burned, its walls torn down, its men exterminated, its women carried away. So even as he licensed Odysseus to give the assurances demanded by Antenor and Aeneas in return for their defection, Agamemnon must have known this was what he would do. He must have been hugging himself with glee when the Trojan defectors accepted those assurances. And why should they not have done when Odysseus had also been deceived?

All his care and craft and guile counted for nothing now. His brain was in flames with the knowledge. If Agamemnon had been standing beside him in that moment Odysseus might have struck him down. But it was another figure that came hurrying towards him out of the night, a huge Ethiopian, one of Memnon's men, half-naked, his black skin glistening with sweat, his eyes wide and very white. Reflexively Odysseus drew his sword and stuck him through the belly.

The shock of the man's weight jarred at his arm, driving the sword deeper. The Ethiopian hung there for a moment impaled, grunting with dismay. Odysseus pulled out the blade and stood back, watching him sag to his knees and fall, shuddering, to the ground. He could hear the black man muttering something in his own tongue – a curse, a gasp of execration, a prayer to whatever gods he served, who knew what those mumblings meant?

Odysseus stared down at the dying man, resentful that he had been drawn into the killing. Then his mind swirled in a blur of rage. If Agamemnon wanted blood, then blood he should have. He advanced across the square towards the sounds of slaughter and once he had begun to kill it seemed there was no stopping. He saw frightened faces gasp and cry as they fell beneath his sword. He saw the wounds splash open. He was killing people swiftly, without compunction, as though doing them a service. At one point he slipped on the entrails of a fat man he had butchered and found himself lying beside him, face to face, with the sightless, outraged eyes staring back into his own. Then he pushed himself to his feet again, driven on by an impulse of disgust, filled with fury and self-loathing.

Almost as deep in delirium as Ajax in his madness had once slaughtered the cattle in their pens, imagining them to be his enemies, Odysseus killed and killed again, working his way through the throng as though convinced that each body that fell before him might prove to be the last, so that he could be liberated, once and for all, from this dreadful duty. His mind was numb. His arm ached from the effort. His throat was parched. It all seemed to be happening in silence.

A Visitor To Ithaca

So loud was the anguish at the fall of Troy you might have thought the noise must carry across the whole astounded world; yet it would be weeks before the news of Agamemnon's victory reached as far as Ithaca. Of all the kingdoms that sent ships to the war, our western islands were furthest from the conflict. We were always last to receive word of how our forces were faring and by the time reports arrived they were far out of date, never at first hand and, more often than not, coloured by rumour and speculation. To make matters worse, Troy was taken late in the year when all the seas were running high and the straits impassable, so the fighting was over long before we got to know of it.

The view must always have been clearer from the high crag at Mycenae but even the intelligence that reached Queen Clytaemnestra was not always reliable, and she was too busy managing Agamemnon's kingdom in his absence to keep my Lady Penelope apprised of events on the eastern seaboard of the Aegean. Meanwhile the infrequent letters Penelope received from her father, Lord Icarius of Sparta, were always terse in their account of a son-in-law of whom he had never approved. So throughout the war we Ithacans were fed on scraps of information that had been picked up in larger ports by traders who came to the island, or that reached us from the occasional deserter who made it back to mainland Argos. Such men had only a fragmentary picture of events, and who could say whether their accounts were trustworthy? All we knew for certain was that Lord Odysseus had still been alive the last time anyone had news of him.

As Prince Telemachus emerged from infancy into the proud knowledge that the father of whom he lacked all memory was one of the great Argive generals, this proved to be an increasingly frustrating state of affairs. So as his friend, I Phemius – still only a boy myself – did what I could to supply his need with flights of my own fanciful imagination. Each day he and I, along with a ragged troupe of fatherless urchins, fought our own version of the Trojan War around the pastures and coves of Ithaca. From hill to hill we launched raids on each other's flocks, singing songs and taking blows. Meanwhile, far away in windy Phrygia, Odysseus used all his guile to steer his comrades towards victory over a foe that had proved tougher and more resilient than anyone but he had anticipated.

Then, in the ninth year of the war we learned that an inconclusive campaign in Mysia had ended with the Argive fleet being blown back to Aulis by a great storm. For a time we lived in the excited hope that Odysseus might seize the chance to visit the wife and child he had left so many years before, but all that came was a long letter which was delivered under seal directly into the hands of Penelope.

The next day she summoned my mother and some of the other women into her presence and with the gentle grace that always distinguished her care for our people, she told them that *The Raven,* the ship in which my father Terpis had sailed from Mysia, had failed to appear at Aulis. There remained a small chance that the crew might have made landfall on one or other of the islands scattered across the Aegean but the women should prepare themselves for the possibility that their husbands were drowned at sea and would not return.

The island rang loud with wailing that day. For me, for a time, it was as though a black gash had been torn in the fabric of things. But remembering how my father, the bard of Ithaca, had sung at the naming day of Prince Telemachus, I converted my fear and grief into a solemn vow that, if he did not return, I would honour his memory by becoming the island's bard myself.

Meanwhile Penelope gave her son as sanguine an account of the letter as she could. How else was she to speak to a ten year old who knew nothing of his father except her love for him and the fact that almost all those he had left behind on the island spoke of him with affection and respect?

Only many years later, long after the war was won and Odysseus still had not returned to Ithaca, was Telemachus allowed to read the letter for himself. He told me that it contained warm expressions both of undying love and of agonized regret that a hard fate had kept him so long from his wife and son. But it was also filled with bitter criticism of the way the war was being fought. In particular, Odysseus was at pains to distance himself from the decision that had just been taken to sacrifice Agamemnon's daughter Iphigenaia on the altar of Artemis in order to secure a fair wind back to Troy.

He attributed the blame for that atrocity to Palamedes, the Prince of Euboea, a man for whom he cherished an abiding hatred. It was Palamedes who had demanded that Odysseus take the terrible oath that had been sworn at Sparta to protect the winner of Helen's hand from the jealousy of his rivals – an oath which Odysseus (who was not a contender for Helen's hand) had himself devised. It had been Palamedes who accompanied Menelaus to Ithaca and compromised Odysseus into joining the war against his will. Now it was Palamedes who had thought up the scheme to lure Iphigenaia to her death in Aulis with the pretence that she was to be married to Achilles, and Odysseus could no longer contain his contempt and loathing for the man's devious mind.

Small wonder then that Penelope had been deeply troubled by the letter, for the roguishly good-humoured, ever-optimistic man she had married was entirely absent from its words. In his place brooded an angry stranger about to return to a war which he had never sought. And he did so with his mind darkened by the conviction that the evil shadow of that war was corrupting all on whom it fell.

So the fleet had put to sea again in the tenth year of the war, and we in Ithaca heard nothing further about the fate of those aboard until the spring afternoon several months later when a black-sailed pentekonter with a serpent figurehead put in at the harbour. It bore the arms of Nauplius, King of Euboea.

Nauplius was not the only visitor to Ithaca at that time. Earlier that week Prince Amphinomus had sailed over from the neighbouring island of Dulichion to pay tribute on behalf of his father, King Nisus, who owed allegiance to Laertes, King of Ithaca. This agreeable young man had proved such an entertaining companion that Penelope persuaded him to remain a while after his business with her father-in-law was done. She claimed that he lifted her spirits in what was, for her, a lonely and anxious time. I also grew fond of Amphinomus. He was possessed of a charming, easy-going manner, was eloquent without showiness, and did not condescend when I revealed in answer to his friendly question that it was my intention to become a bard like my father before me. But Telemachus took against him from the first and to such a degree that his mother felt obliged to admonish the boy for his rudeness.

'Don't be too hard on him,' Amphinomus mildly chided her. 'After all, he has lacked the guidance of his father's hand.'

'Sons have lost their fathers in this war and fathers their sons,' Penelope sighed. 'Sometimes I can see no end to the woes it brings.'

'My own father feels the same way.' Amphinomus gave her a wry smile. 'He often thanks the gods that I was too young to go to Troy with Odysseus – though there have been times when I bitterly reproached them for the same reason.'

'Well, I pray that the war will be over long before you are called upon to serve,' Penelope replied, 'and not least so that my husband will come back soon to take this skittish colt of mine in hand.'

At which remark Telemachus scowled, whistled his father's dog Argus to his heel, and left the chamber.

'Go with him, Phemius.' Penelope favoured me with the smile that always made my heart swim. 'See if you can't improve his ill humour before we dine.'

But when I did as I was bidden, Telemachus merely glowered at me. 'You should have stayed and kept an eye on him,' he said. 'I don't trust that man. He's too eager to be liked.'

'I like him well enough anyway,' I said. 'He's asked me to sing for him tonight.'

But Telemachus was already staring out to sea where the distant sail of an approaching ship bulged like a black patch stitched into the glittering blue-green. 'Who's this putting in now?' he murmured, throwing a stone into the swell. 'No doubt some other itchy hound come sniffing at my mother's skirts.'

Until that moment such a thought had never crossed my mind. Penelope was the faithful wife of the Lord Odysseus and everyone knew that theirs was a love-match. While most of the other princes of Argos had lusted after Helen, Odysseus remained constant in his devotion to her Spartan cousin, the daughter of Icarius. Their marriage had been a cause for great joy on Ithaca and though its early years had been shadowed by a grievous number of miscarriages, no one doubted that the shared grief had deepened their love, or that it was only with the most anguished reluctance that Odysseus finally left his wife and newborn son to fight in the war at Troy. Then, as the war dragged on and King Laertes and his queen Anticleia grew older, Penelope had become the graceful Lady of the island. She was always a reliable source of comfort and wisdom to those in need, revered throughout all Argos for her constancy, and utterly beyond reproach. So I don't know whether I was more shocked by the vehemence of what Telemachus had said or troubled by my sense of its astuteness.

I was fifteen years old at that time. Telemachus was four years younger, yet he had seen what my own innocently cherished infatuation had failed to see – that the fate of Odysseus was at best uncertain and if he failed to return to Ithaca then Penelope would become the most desirable of prizes. I also realized in that moment that if Telemachus had seen it, then others must have seen it too. And with that thought it occurred to me that he must have overheard someone else uttering some such remark as the one he had just made. In any case, my angry friend stood scowling out to sea, too young to defend his mother's honour but not too young to worry over it.

However the black ship bearing down on our island that day did not carry some hopeful suitor making a speculative bid for Penelope but someone more devious – a bitter old man motivated neither by love nor by lust but by an inveterate hatred, which he did not at first reveal.

I clearly remember King Nauplius coming ashore on the island that day – a scraggy, bald-headed figure in his sixties with a hawkish nose and an elaborately barbered beard. There was a gaunt and flinty cast to his features, and the shadows webbed around his eyes darkened the critical regard with which he studied both our undefended harbour and the homely palace on the cliff. But what most impressed my young imagination were the conspicuous mourning robes he wore. I remember thinking that whatever news this king was bringing, it could not be good.

King Laertes, the father of Odysseus, was not present in the palace to receive this unexpected visitor. In those days the old king had taken to spending more and more time tending the crops and animals on his farm, or simply sitting in the shade, fanning himself with his hat and wishing that his son would return from the foreign war to assume the burden of kingship over the western islands. Laertes had been famous among the heroes of Argos in his day. As a young man, he had sailed to far Colchis with Jason on the raid that brought back the Golden Fleece. He was also among those who hunted the great boar that Divine

Artemis had loosed to ravage the lands around Calydon, but he was growing old and weary now. Earlier that week he had received the year's tribute from Dulichion, Same and Zacynthus, and then done what he could to give fair judgement over the various disputes that had arisen between them while their leaders were away. Now, once more, he had retreated with his wife Anticleia to the peace of his farm.

Having apologized to the unexpected royal visitor for the king's absence, Penelope was ordering a runner to call Laertes back to court when Nauplius raised a restraining hand and gravely shook his head. 'There is no need to trouble him,' he said. 'Let old Laertes enjoy such peace as this world allows. In any case, it is you I have come to see.'

The words fell on the air as stark and grim as the robes he wore. Sensing that grief had turned to a mortal sickness inside the man, Penelope said, 'I see you have suffered some great loss, my lord.' But she was remembering how she herself had suffered at the last visit from the royal house of Euboea. Already she was fearful that the ill news that Nauplius brought with him must press closely on her own life too.

'A loss from which I do not expect to recover,' Nauplius answered. 'This war has cost me my son.'

'Palamedes is dead?'

The grey eyes studied her as if in reproach. 'You have had no word from Troy?'

'We have heard nothing since the fleet sailed from Aulis.' Opening helpless hands, Penelope shook her head. 'I grieve to hear of your loss. Tell me, how did this thing happen?'

Nauplius made as if to answer, then seemed to change his mind, shaking his head at the immense burden of what he had to utter. 'I have sailed far today,' he sighed, 'and my heart is heavy with evil tidings. Let me first rest a while and regain my strength. Then we shall speak of the grief that this war has brought to us.' Nodding with the absolute authority of a sovereign who had decided that everything that needed to be said for the time being had now been said, he turned away, raising a ringed hand to his body-servant for support.

'Of course,' Penelope answered uneasily. 'My steward will escort you to your chamber. But first . . . Forgive me, but I must ask you, Lord Nauplius . . .'

Frowning, the old king tilted his head to look back at her. Penelope forced herself to speak. 'Do you have word of my husband?' She saw how one flinty eye was narrower than the other and its lid quivered like a moth beneath its brow. Into a silence that had gone on too long she said, 'Does Odysseus live?'

Nauplius drew in his breath and stood with his mottled head nodding still.

'Oh yes,' the voice was barely more than a hoarse wheeze, 'Odysseus lives still. Odysseus lives.' And again, with a sigh that seemed to rebuke the relief that broke visibly across her face, he turned away.

When Nauplius and his attendants had left the hall, Amphinomus approached Penelope, smiling. 'Good news at last, my lady.'

'Yes.' Penelope stood with the fingertips of her right hand at her cheek. 'But I fear that Nauplius has more to say.'

Amphinomus shrugged. 'It may only be that his grief has darkened his view of things. You mustn't let his shadow dim your own fair light.'

Penelope shook her head. 'The truth is that I didn't greatly care for Palamedes. He was a clever man, in some ways as clever as Odysseus, but he lacked warmth. And I have often wished that he had never set foot on this island. If he hadn't come here with Menelaus all those years ago, Telemachus would have a father to watch over him and I a husband in my bed. Yet one must pity any man who has lost his son.'

'One must indeed,' Amphinomus pursed his lips, 'even though he brings a deathly chill into the hall with him!'

Penelope reproved the arch smile in the young man's hand-some face. 'It wouldn't surprise me to learn that the King of

Euboea sickens from more than grief. Also he is as much a guest of the house as you are, sir. We will be civil with him.' But she was glad of her friend's company in what threatened to be a difficult and demanding time.

Her apprehensions were confirmed at dinner that evening when Nauplius merely frowned in response to Penelope's warmly expressed hope that he was well rested, and then went on to express his surprise that a young woman of the royal house of Sparta had not long since grown discontented with the dull round of life in rustic Ithaca.

'I regret that our plain ways are not to your taste,' Penelope answered. 'I myself have always found the simple life here wonderfully refreshing after the rivalries and gossip of the court in Sparta. With each day that passes I learn to love this island and its people more.' Nor did she entirely conceal the reproach in her voice as she added, 'Indeed I sometimes think that were all the world to emulate such dullness, it might be a happier and more peaceful place.'

'Your husband has been gone for nearly ten years, madam,' Nauplius replied. 'Have those years not taught you that happiness and peace are not to be found anywhere for long?'

Penelope shrugged her delicate shoulders. 'I respect the wisdom of your years, my lord, but it may be that Ithaca has something to teach you still.'

'However,' Amphinomus put in, 'we are all eager for news of the war, and not much reaches us here. Will you share with us what you know of its progress?'

'Troy still stands,' Nauplius glowered. 'Men fight beneath its walls and die, and it would seem that Agamemnon and Achilles are fiercer in their quarrels with each other than they are with the Trojans. Meanwhile prudent counsel is ignored and honest men are traduced by liars. In short, the Argive army is led by knaves and fools. What more is there to say?' Undismayed by the flush he had brought to Penelope's face, he looked away.

Amphinomus said quietly, 'I think you forget that Lord Odysseus is among those who command the host.'

'No, sir, I do not forget,' Nauplius answered shortly.

From further down the table Lord Mentor, whom Odysseus had entrusted with the management of his affairs on Ithaca uttered a low growl. 'Then you will except him from your remarks, I trust?'

But either Nauplius did not hear him or affected not to have done so. He took a trial sip from his wine-cup, wrinkled his nostrils in a barely concealed grimace of disappointment, and smiled at Penelope. 'Our Euboean vintage is mellower, my dear. I must make a point of sending you some.'

Her voice uncharacteristically tense, Penelope said, 'My husband is no man's fool, sir. Do you suggest he is a knave?'

Nauplius opened his hands in a mild gesture of protest. 'You were daughter to my old friend Icarius long before you became wife to Odysseus. Believe me, I have no desire to say anything that would cause you pain or displeasure.'

Aware that the answer was neither a withdrawal nor an apology, Penelope made an effort to still her breathing. If she had suspected earlier that this dour old man had come with mischief at work in his embittered mind, she was convinced of it now. Looking for space to gather her thoughts, she turned to Amphinomus. 'Did you not ask Phemius to sing for you tonight? Perhaps his voice will please our royal guest?'

And so I was required to stand before this uneasy table and raise my voice in the silence. I had been looking forward to this moment all day but any bard will tell you that few can sing at their best before those whose minds are elsewhere. My ambition had been to sing from *The Lay of Lord Odysseus* on which I had been working, and in the circumstances it would have been the courageous thing to do. But I was reluctant to expose a still raw and tender talent before a judge as stern as King Nauplius, so I chose instead to sing some of the traditional goat-songs sung by shepherds on the island. Amphinomus and Lady Penelope received them warmly enough, but those bucolic airs appealed no more to the visiting king's ears than our island's wine had done to his palate.

'My son told me that you liked to keep a simple life here on Ithaca,' he said dryly, 'but I'm surprised to find that the court of Laertes lacks a bard even!'

'The boy's father is our bard,' Penelope answered quietly. 'There is some fear that his life was lost at sea after the Mysian campaign.'

'A campaign against which my own son strongly advised,' Nauplius said with narrowed eyes, 'but other counsel was preferred, and with what disastrous results we may all now plainly see.' Then he cast a searching look my way. 'The boy sings sweetly enough,' he conceded. 'I hear the grief in his voice. It is hard for a son to lose a father, but it is in the natural course of things.' Nauplius shook his gaunt head. 'For a father to lose a son however . . .'

Amphinomus said, 'Surely a father can take comfort from the knowledge that his son died honourably in battle?'

But Nauplius turned a cold stare on him. 'My son was denied such honour. And denied it by those whom he had loyally sought to serve.'

The silence was broken by Lord Mentor. 'As the king has observed,' he said, 'we are simple souls on Ithaca. Perhaps he will make his meaning plainer.'

Nauplius met the controlled anger with a bleak smile. 'In good time,' he said, 'in good time. My business here is with the Lady Penelope. If she will grant me private audience when this meal is done, we will talk more of these things.'

'You are the guest of our house,' Penelope answered. 'It shall be as you wish.'

And so, with the only subjects about which people wished to speak thus firmly confined to silence, this awkward meal progressed. Amphinomus did what he could to ease the atmosphere by extolling the contribution that Euboea had made to the art of navigation. In particular he praised that island's introduction of cliff-top beacons beside dangerous shoals, an invention which had caught on across Argive waters and proved a boon to mariners everywhere.

Nauplius nodded in acknowledgement. He and Amphinomus chatted together for a while. 'It pleases me,' he said, 'to learn that the Lady Penelope has found a diverting companion in her husband's absence.' And at the fireside pillar where we sat with the dog Argus stretched between us, kicking his hind-legs in a dream of chase, I saw Telemachus scowl.

Eventually, having eaten well for all his disdain for rustic fare, Nauplius declared himself replete, washed his hands in the bronze bowl and indicated his desire to speak alone with the lady of the house. We watched them leave the hall together, he gaunt and frail, she taller by almost a head, yet they felt worryingly like an executioner and his victim.

'Come, Phemius,' Amphinomus called across the hall, 'sing for us again.'

Not for many years, not indeed till after her husband's return, did Penelope utter a word about what was said between her and King Nauplius that night. The following morning, shortly after dawn, that disagreeable visitor put out to sea without offering thanks or saying farewell to anyone. No one on the island regretted his departure though we were all troubled by the shadow that he had evidently cast across Penelope's mind and face, and not even Amphinomus could persuade her to share the burden of her cares.

Not many weeks would pass, of course, before we learned that this was only one of many visits that Nauplius was to make to the chief kingdoms of Argos, and everywhere he went, including, most dramatically, Mycenae itself, he left the contamination of his vengeful grief. And from reports of what happened elsewhere it was not difficult to guess what must have passed between Nauplius and Penelope that night.

Nauplius would have begun by singing the praises of his dead son Palamedes. Was his not the swiftest and most orderly mind in the Argive leadership? Had he not come to the aid of the duller-witted Agamemnon by recommending an order of battle which would take full advantage of the diverse forces assembled under his command rather than allowing their rivalries and customs to weaken their strength and cause disarray? Had he not devised a common signalling system that could be understood and exploited equally well by tribesmen from Arcadia, Crete, Boeotia and Magnesia? Had he not unified the systems of measurement used throughout the host so that there could be no confusion over distances and arguments over the distribution of rations and booty might be kept to a minimum? Wasn't it Palamedes who had kept the troops in good heart by teaching them his game of dice and stones? Hadn't he always done what he could to make sure that the voice of the common soldiery was heard among the council of the kings? In short, Nauplius insisted that if it had not been for the presiding intelligence of Palamedes, anticipating difficulties and finding means to overcome them, Agamemnon's vast army would quickly have degenerated into a quarrelsome rabble with each tribal contingent looking only to its own interests even though the entire campaign might founder on such narrow pride.

Penelope would have listened patiently to all of this. After all, the man was her house-guest and it was understandable that a father's grief should exaggerate his dead son's contribution to the arduous effort of a war in which he'd lost his life. She had no doubt, of course, that the intelligence and experience of Odysseus must have played at least an equal part in that effort, and probably a greater one, but she had already sensed that to speak up for her husband at this juncture could only arouse a hostile response from this lugubrious old man. So she preferred to hold her peace and wait to see what menace still lay concealed behind his show of grief.

It was not long in coming. Frowning into space as he spoke, Nauplius told how, late in the previous year, when their supplies began to dwindle and raids along the Phrygian and Thracian coasts produced little by way of grain and stores, the Argive host had been faced with a choice between starving outside the walls of Troy or turning tail with little to show for all those long years of war. Odysseus had been in command of one of the raiding parties that returned with its holds empty. When he was met by the rage of Agamemnon, he publicly defied any man to do better. The harvests had failed everywhere that year, he claimed. The granaries were bare.

'Palamedes took up the challenge,' Nauplius said, 'and when he returned to the camp only a few days later, his ships rode low in the water, heavy with grain. You would have thought he deserved the heartfelt thanks of the entire host, would you not? And the common soldiers were warm enough in their praise. My son had always championed their cause. Now he had saved them from hunger. But with the generals it was a different story.' Fiercely the old man drew in his breath. 'Whenever there had been conflict among them as to the most effective course of action, Palamedes was invariably proved right. The high command sometimes paid a high price in blood for ignoring his advice and now, once again, my son had succeeded where others had failed. Their envy turned first to spite and then to malice. At least one of them was determined to blacken his name.'

By now Penelope must already have guessed the direction of Nauplius's story. She knew very well that Odysseus cared for Palamedes no more than she did herself. But nothing could have prepared her for the charge that Nauplius was about to bring against her husband.

'My son used to send me frequent reports of the progress of the war,' he said. 'After all, I had been one of Agamemnon's principal backers from the first. To fight this war he needed the wealth of Euboea as well as our ships. Without the huge loans I made him, he could never have mustered half the force he did. And both my son and I were well aware that those loans would not be repaid unless Troy fell. So Palamedes went to the war as the guardian of my investment. I relied on him to make sure that the campaign was effectively pursued. I relied on him for news. When he fell silent I began to suspect that something untoward had happened.' After a grim silence Nauplius said, 'I sent urgent messages to the Atreides brothers. When no word came back I decided to sail for Phrygia myself.'

After a deliberate silence Penelope asked, 'And what did you learn there?'

'I learned that my son had been dead for some time. But he had been denied an honourable death in battle. Palamedes had been traduced by men he took to be his friends. Envious men. Men who worked in darkness to do him harm. A conspiracy of lies had been mounted against him. He was accused of treason. Evidence was fabricated. It purported to show that he had taken Trojan bribes. He was tried and found guilty by the very men who had perpetrated this foul calumny. Palamedes, always the most prudent and honourable of men, met a traitor's end. He was stoned to death by the host he had sought to serve to the very best of his ability.' Nauplius was shaking as he spoke. His lips quivered but his eyes were dry as in a hoarse whisper he said, 'My son's last words were, "Truth, I mourn for you, who have predeceased me."'

The words lay heavily on the silence for a time. They could hear the sound of men carousing in the hall below. Eventually Penelope raised her eyes. 'You are impugning the honour of Agamemnon and Menelaus?' she demanded.

'I am,' Nauplius answered, 'and I am impugning Diomedes of Tiryns and Idomeneus of Crete who conspired with them against my son.' He paused to fix her with his flinty stare. 'And I am impugning your husband Odysseus who was the father of these lies.'

'Then I will hear no more of this,' Penelope said steadily, 'for it seems to me that anyone can vilify another man's name when he is not present to defend himself, but there can be no honour in such slander.'

'Which is precisely what your husband did to my son,' Nauplius retorted, 'and his shade still cries out for justice. Do not turn away from me, Penelope. I have never felt anything other than affection in my heart for you. Yet I confess I have long shared your father's doubts about the man you chose for your husband. Odysseus was always a plausible rogue, yes, but a rogue nevertheless. And now I know him to be more and worse than a rogue – he is a villain, one who will stoop to any deceit to secure his own ends. Do not turn away, my dear, for as you will soon learn to your bitter cost, you are as much the victim of his duplicity as I have been.'

But Penelope was already on her feet and crossing the room to leave it. She stopped at the door to confront the old man with the cold rebuke of her eyes. 'You have already said too much.'

'The truth is often painful, I know,' he began to answer, 'but it must be heard if justice is to be done.'

'You are the guest of my husband's house,' Penelope interrupted him, 'and you are also old, sir. So I will not ask you to leave this place at once. But I advise you to take to your ship at dawn. Otherwise I will not answer for your safety.'

'Hear me,' Nauplius beseeched as she turned to open the door. 'I speak only out of care for you. This war has corrupted all who lead it. Why do you imagine that not one of them has come home in all these years? It is not because they are constantly in the field, I assure you. Far from it! Those errant gentlemen have long been living a life of licence and debauchery out there in Phrygia. From all the many women they have taken to their tents, each has now selected his favourite concubine. And there is more. They mean to make queens of their oriental paramours when they return to Argos. Pledges have been given before the gods. Believe me, my dear, Odysseus is as faithless as the rest.' He took in the hostile glitter of Penelope's eyes and refused to be abashed by it. 'You do well to look for comfort elsewhere. Amphinomus is a handsome fellow.'

Penelope drew in her breath. 'Now I am sure that you lie,' she said. 'May the gods forgive you for it, for I cannot. Let me never see your face on Ithaca again.'

She left the chamber, banging the door behind her. Yet for all her defiance I doubt that she slept that night. Nor can she have known much rest in the days and nights that followed, for secrets and lies are defilers of the heart and once the trust of the heart is breached it knows no peace. So Penelope was often to be heard sighing as she worked her loom by day, or again when she made her offerings to Athena and prayed that the goddess might teach her patience of soul. And often she would walk alone along the cliff, gazing out to sea as she wondered what had happened to her husband beneath the distant walls of Troy.

The Division of the Spoils

Dawn, when it finally came, was little more than a ruddy gleam blackened by smoke and made redder by the flames still rising from the burning buildings. Again and again throughout the night the nerves of the Trojan women had been shaken by the noise of roof-beams collapsing and the harsh clatter of falling tiles. Here and there the hoarse gust of a blaze still sent its vivid exhaust of sparks upwards through the smoke, but most of the fires were now under control, all resistance had ended, and only occasional screams rose from men under torment to reveal where their riches were concealed.

The streets stank vilely of blood and excrement. With the trap-door still hanging open at its belly, the wooden horse looked down on a dense litter of corpses. Already kites and vultures circled. Somewhere, indifferent to everything but the glory of his own existence, a cockerel crowed his clarion to the day.

A few of the women had briefly taken refuge in oblivion, but only Cassandra had truly slept that night, and it would have been wrong to deduce from the subdued sound of their sobbing that the captives were calmer now. Rather, with the coming of the light, they felt more than ever to be the victims of a fate so violent and capricious that it numbed their frightened minds. Yesterday Troy had been intact behind its walls, having withstood all the strength the Argive host could bring against it. Today the city was a ruin and its royal women were waiting like stockyard cattle to be apportioned among foreigners they detested and feared.

Yet the sun seemed content to preside over such outrageous fortune and the sky might have been void of gods for all the notice it took of their imprecations. So these women were far from calm. They huddled together, exiled from the past, afraid of the future, seeking from each other the solace that none had to give, and deprived even of the means to kill themselves.

Polyxena crouched among them, knowing that sooner or later Neoptolemus must come in search of her again. She had been present by the altar of Zeus when that terrifying youth had struck off her father's head, and she had guessed already that he would seek her out. The sixteen year old girl had huddled behind her sister Laodice in the portico earlier that night, listening to his voice cajoling her to reveal herself. She had cast about for a form of words that might convince him that she had been only the unwitting bait in the trap that had been set for Achilles. But she had seen the torchlight glancing off his sword and knew that words would make no difference. The boy was fanatical in his desire to avenge his father. Her only chance of survival was to conceal herself among the other women in the hope that he might be struck down by the hand of a merciful god before he could identify her. Then, when Agamemnon had called Neoptolemus away, she had begun to wonder whether the fates might prove kindly after all. But as the night wore on there was no evidence of kindness in this stricken city and when daylight broke, her terror returned with greater force.

Polyxena could not prevent her teeth from chattering as she crouched beside her mother who sat nursing Andromache's head in her lap. Beside them Cassandra whispered prophecies that the Trojans would prove more fortunate than their enemies. They had at least died in defence of their sacred homeland, while thousands of the barbarian invaders had perished far from their homes, and those who made it back to Argos would find a cruel fate waiting for them.

'Agamemnon will see that he has taken death into his bed,' Cassandra chanted. 'Already the lioness couples with the goat. A blade glints in the bath-house. A torrent of blood flows there. I too shall be swept away on that red tide. But the son of Agamemnon shall bring a bloody end to Neoptolemus. He will leave his impious body dead beneath Apollo's stone. As for that ingenious fiend Odysseus, Blue-haired Poseidon will keep him far from the home while others junket and riot in his hall. The Goddess will seize his heart. Hades will open his dark door to him. Death will crowd his house.' But none of the women believed the mad girl any more than they could silence her. So they sat together under the portico, watching the sun come up and dreading what the day must bring.

Exhausted from the efforts of the night, most of the Argive leaders were relaxing in the palace across the square. The first elation of victory had passed and the rush of wine to their heads brought, at that early hour, only a queasy sense of what they had achieved. Odysseus had wandered off alone somewhere. Apart from Menelaus, who still brooded in the mansion that Paris had built for Helen, the others were carousing together, but there were grumbles of dissent from Acamas and his brother Demophon when Neoptolemus claimed the right to take Polyxena for his own before the lots had been apportioned.

Annoyed that even in this hour of triumph, discord should have broken out so quickly among his followers, Agamemnon stood uncertainly. He knew there was some justice in the complaint but he was reluctant to offend Neoptolemus who had shown a ferocity in the fight against the Ethiopians that had astounded older, battle-hardened men. Also he knew what fate lay in store for Polyxena if he acceded to this demand, and his thoughts had involuntarily darkened at the memory of what he had done to his own daughter Iphigenaia.

Seeing his hesitation, Neoptolemus declared that the shade of his father had demanded in a dream that the girl who had betrayed him should be sacrificed on his tomb. 'Does the High King not believe that the man who did so much to win this war should be accorded such justice? Would you deny my father's shade?'

Immediately Agamemnon made the sign to ward off the evil eye. A quarrel with Achilles had almost lost him this war once. He would not risk another with his angry ghost. 'Take her,' he said. 'It is only just.'

So Neoptolemus came to claim Polyxena in the early morning light. Again he summoned her out of the huddle of women. Again Hecuba rose to protect her youngest daughter. But the weary young warrior was in no mood to listen to her pleas and insults. 'If you don't want to feel the flat of my sword on your old bones,' he snarled, 'tell your daughter to show herself.'

Polyxena rose from the place where she had been crouching. 'I am here,' she declared in a voice that shook as she spoke. 'Achilles asked for me more gently. If you hope to emulate your father, you must learn to speak with something other than your sword.'

'Come into the light,' Neoptolemus answered. 'Let me take a look at you.'

Loosing the hand of Laodice, Polyxena stepped between the women huddled round her and stared without flinching at the youth. Being his senior by three years or more, she might, in other circumstances, have taunted him for parading in the suit of armour that had been made to fit his father's broader shoulders. But she knew that her life stood in graver danger now than when she had met with Achilles in Apollo's temple at Thymbra. Her face was flushed with fear. Her breath was drawn too quickly. When Neoptolemus smiled at the swift rise and fall of her recently budded breasts she glanced away.

'I understand that my father sought to befriend you,' he said. 'Is that not so?'

'Achilles asked to speak with me, yes.'

'But it was you who made the first approach.'

Nervously she whispered, 'My father asked it of me.' Polyxena's gaze had been fixed on the ground beneath her. Now she looked up hopelessly into those cold eyes. 'We thought it the only hope of having Hector's body returned to us.'

'And because my father had a noble heart he acceded to that hope, did he not?'

Polyxena nodded and averted her eyes.

'Yet that was not the last time you saw him?'

Her arms were crossed at her breast. Now she was trembling so much that she could barely speak. 'But it was Achilles who sought me out.'

'Perhaps you had given him cause to do so?'

'I swear not,' she gasped. 'The priest told me he had come looking for me many times. The thought of it frightened me. I didn't understand what he wanted.'

'But still you came.'

'Yes.'

'And you didn't come alone. You told your treacherous brother Paris that Achilles was to be found unguarded at the temple of Apollo. You told him exactly when he would be there. You told him to bring his bow and kill my father in vengeance for the death of your brother Hector.'

'That is not how it was!' Polyxena cried.

But Neoptolemus was not listening. He was remembering that Odysseus had told him how, in a quiet hour together, Achilles had confessed his tender feelings for Polyxena. Looking at the girl now – the tousled ringlets blowing about her face, the delicate hands at her shoulders, the shape of her slim thighs disclosed by the pull of the breeze at her shift – he thought he understood how this alluring combination of poise and vulnerability might have tugged at his father's heart.

It did so now, seditiously, at his own.

Yet this girl had betrayed his father, whose shade cried out for vengeance.

'And is not Thymbra under the protection of the god?' he

demanded. 'Isn't it a sacred place of truce where men from both sides – Argive and Trojan alike – were free to make their offerings without fear?'

Seeing that her truth and his must forever lie far from each other's reach, Polyxena lowered her head again and consigned herself to silence.

Accusation gathered force in his voice. 'But you and your brothers lacked all reverence for the god. Together you violated the sanctuary of Apollo's temple. Your brothers were afraid to face my father in open combat like true men, so they set a trap for him. And you, daughter of Priam, were the willing bait in that trap.'

In a low whisper Polyxena said, 'I knew nothing of what they planned.'

Neoptolemus snorted. 'I think you're lying to me – as you lied to my father before me. I think, daughter of Priam, that it's time you were purified of lies.'

He turned away from her and gestured to the two Myrmidons who stood at his back. The women who had listened with pent breath to their tense exchanges began to moan and whimper as the Myrmidons stepped forward to seize Polyxena by her thin arms.

Swaying where she stood, Hecuba screeched, 'Where are you taking her?'

'To my father's tomb,' Neoptolemus answered coldly. 'There is a last service she can perform for him there.' Then all the women were wailing again as they watched Polyxena dragged off through the gritty wind blowing across the square, past the impassive effigy of the horse, towards the Scaean Gate.

Walking at dawn through ransacked streets where only the dead were gathered, Odysseus disturbed vultures and pie-dogs already tugging at the silent piles of human flesh. They cowered at his approach or flapped away on verminous wings, peevishly watching as he stared at the horror of what had been done.

During the course of the night a living city had been transformed into a vast necropolis. Its very air was charred and excremental. As though some swift, inexorable pestilence had struck out of the night sky, all its men folk had lain down in droves, their necks gaudy with wounds, their entrails flowering in garlands from their bellies, their eyes gaping at the day. Here lay a man who might once have been a jolly butcher, now with his ribs split open like a side of beef. There, in a slovenly mess, crouched two twin boys – they could only recently have learned to speak – with their infant brains dashed out against a wall. And over there a youth sat propped against an almond tree, evidently puzzled by the broken blade of a sword that had been left protruding like a handle from his skull. And still, in the boughs of that tree, a linnet sang.

When he came out into a small square strewn with bodies, Odysseus saw three men who had followed him to Troy from Dulichion. They were quenching their thirst at a fountain while another milked a nanny-goat into an upturned helmet clutched between his knees. Across the square a half-naked woman with blood splashed at her thighs sat weeping in the doorway of a house.

The soldiers leapt to their feet at his approach, pressing knuckles to their brows as though expecting a reprimand. When Odysseus merely asked if he might share their water, he was offered goat's milk but said that water was all he wanted. Before he could reach the fountain however, the weary men relaxed and began to congratulate him on the success of his ruse. Only a man out of the Ionian isles, they declared, could have been canny enough to dream up a scheme as clever as that of the wooden horse.

'We shall have tales to tell when we get home, sir,' lisped the oldest of them, a grey-headed man who had taken a scar across his mouth and lost half his teeth in the rout at the palisade much earlier that year.

'Do you think there was ever a night of slaughter such as this?' asked another.

Odysseus shook his head, unspeaking.

The man who had been milking the goat said, 'There's been times I've wondered whether I'd ever get to see my wife again, but thanks to you, sir, I expect to come home a rich man now.'

The first man nodded, grinning. 'It seems the gods were with us after all.'

Around them, the bodies of the dead paid scant attention to these ordinary men, their murderers. And when Odysseus opened his mouth he found he could not speak. His hands were trembling again. When he lifted them to where water splashed in the basin of the fountain he realized that his arms were still stained with blood up to his elbows.

Hurriedly he washed them clean, then cupped his hands at the spout and lifted them to his lips. Water splashed across his tongue like light. He stood swaying a moment, possessed by brief startling intimations of another life in which, with a frenzy entirely alien to his nature, he too had joined the massacre. He saw the Ethiopian mumbling in his blood; he saw the fat man's eyes staring back at him.

Then he returned to time. He heard the water splashing in the bowl and the woman sobbing still.

Nodding at the soldiers with a weary, distracted smile, Odysseus walked out of the square towards the gate, making for the sea.

At a wind-blown dune not far from the burial mound of Achilles he came to a halt and stood alone beside the sea, watching a flight of pelicans flag their way across the bay. Then his gaze shifted westwards with such concentration that his keen eyesight might have travelled out across the turbulent Aegean and over the mountains of Thessaly to focus on his small homestead island of Ithaca. He was thinking about his wife Penelope and his little son Telemachus, who must now be almost as old as Neoptolemus. With a fervour that amazed him, Odysseus heard himself praying that, unlike the son of Achilles, his own boy would never rejoice in a night of slaughter such as the one he had just endured.

Hunched against the wind, he remembered the dream that had

come to him on Ithaca – the furrows of his fields sown with salt, his infant son thrown down before the ploughshare. Ten years, the sibyl at the Earth-mother's shrine had said, ten wasted years must pass before Troy fell. And now Troy had fallen, destroyed by his own ingenuity, and those long years of war seemed waste indeed, for he had lost more in a single night than all the gold of Troy could redeem. He had done such things as would chill his wife's blood should she ever come to hear of them.

The white caps of the breakers rolling in off the Hellespont clashed against the shore. The wind banged about his ears. Odysseus swayed where he stood. His breathing was irregular, his tongue dry as a stone in his mouth. Shivering, he lifted a hand to his brow and found that his temples were rimed with sweat. His fingers trembled. He sensed that his nerves had begun at last to mutiny.

He had been standing alone by the clamour of the sea for perhaps an hour when he saw the small party making its way towards the burial mound of Achilles. Two lightly armoured Myrmidons were pushing along the slight figure of a girl whose hair was winnowed by the breeze. Clutching a blanket about her shoulders, she trod the shingle gingerly in bare feet. Behind them walked a smallish warrior in a golden breastplate: Neoptolemus.

Instantly Odysseus knew what the youth intended to do. In the same moment Neoptolemus recognized him and called out that Agamemnon had been asking for him. 'The division of the spoils will take place soon,' he said. 'Let me do what I have to do, then we can walk back together.'

Shielding his eyes against the glare from the sun, Odysseus said, 'Is that Polyxena you have there?'

'The whore that betrayed my father, yes. I mean to sacrifice her on his tomb. Come and stand witness.'

'Have you questioned her?' Odysseus demanded. 'Have you heard her side of the story?'

Neoptolemus frowned at his comrade across the space between

them. 'She claims she had no idea what Paris and Deiphobus were up to. But then she would say that, wouldn't she?'

'It may be the truth,' Odysseus urged. 'Think about it. You don't want innocent blood on your hands. Your father was fond of her. He gave me reason to think that Polyxena was fond of him too.'

'Such are the wiles of women. She's tried the same game with me. The bitch is all temptation.' Neoptolemus spat onto the sand. 'Are you coming or not?'

Odysseus looked across to where the girl stood desolate in the morning light, He found himself remembering Iphigenaia on the altar at Aulis – how she had been brought to her death on the pretence that she was to be married to Achilles. Then he was thinking of Deidameia, the mother of the baby who was to become Neoptolemus, and how bitterly she had grieved when Achilles left Skyros. And then about Briseis, over whom Achilles had quarrelled with Agamemnon in a dispute that almost wrecked the Argive cause. Whenever Achilles let his fierce radiance fall on a woman it seemed that disaster must ensue, as though he had inherited his mother's glamour like a curse. Yet above all Odysseus was thinking about his own wife and what judgement she would pass on a man who stood by and watched a helpless girl dragged to her death by a half-demented boy.

He looked up and saw Polyxena staring at him. Where he might have expected to find a desperate appeal in her eyes, he saw only the glazed terror of a trapped hare. The world was an immense snare, and she was caught in it, and struggle was of no avail.

'Let her go, Neoptolemus,' he shouted.

When only a dubious silence came in reply, he added, 'I'll buy her from you if you like, out of my own share in the spoils.'

'Fancy her yourself, do you?'

Odysseus shook his head in pained incredulity. 'I can't believe that your father would want this.'

'Oh but you're wrong.' Neoptolemus smiled. 'He came to me in a dream. He told me that his shade would know no rest until the whore who betrayed him lay dead on his tomb.'

Odysseus stared across at that fanatical young face, already aware that nothing he could say or do would ever penetrate such certainty. 'But you never knew your father,' he protested. 'You were too young. How can you be sure it was him in your dream and not just some shadow of your own rage?'

Neoptolemus merely jeered again. 'And I thought you were the one who put his trust in dreams.' With a flash of sunlight off his breastplate, he turned away, ordering his men to push the girl on towards the top of the great mound where his father's ashes lay buried in a golden urn, mingled with those of Achilles' beloved friend Patroclus.

Odysseus stood trembling as he watched them go. Having always prided himself on his ingenuity, his resourcefulness, his intelligence, he saw in those moments that he possessed no more than a callow understanding of the aptitude for evil lurking in human nature, doggedly awaiting its chance to thrive. And the failure was a failure of self-understanding also, for as the past night had just shown he was in no way exempt from this terrible propensity. Yet after ten years of war, he remained, it seemed, the merest novice in those ordeals of anguish through which deep wisdom might be learned; and if he had been so easily made Agamemnon's dupe, it was only because for far too long he had duped himself, proclaiming things in which he had no belief, acting as he had no wish to act, capering before the world as a clever, but morally derelict, cipher of a man.

Overwhelmed by a stultifying sense of his own futility, Odysseus knew that what he was about to see must be seared for ever on his mind, but he lacked the will even to avert his eyes. When the figures reached the summit of the mound, he saw the girl pushed roughly to the ground. He could hear nothing, for if words were spoken, the wind snatched them away. He saw Neoptolemus draw his sword, but before he could raise it to strike, Polyxena got to her feet. She stood with the wind wrapping her thin dress taut about her limbs, lifted her chin, and tore open the cloth at her chest so that her small breasts and neck were bared. Momentarily

Neoptolemus seemed disconcerted by the act. Her pride, her refusal to be cowed, must have struck him as impertinence. To his strict mind there was something shameless in the way she flaunted before his sword. It was as if she was choosing death as her lover in preference to him. Then with a curt tilt of her head Polyxena swept her hair back and lengthened her neck before the blade. Her eyes remained open. Odysseus felt sure that she was looking precisely in his direction as the sword sliced through the air.

Meanwhile an urgent, increasingly ill-tempered restlessness had possessed the victorious host. Most of them wanted to get away as quickly as possible from a place where evidence of their crimes lay rife around them. Already the air was tainted with the stink of decaying flesh. Soon it must prove insufferable. Yet after those years of struggle, each man was determined to grab as much as he could before leaving and there was a prodigious bounty of loot in the captured city.

In the early hours of the sack, a gang of Lapiths caught pillaging a small temple on their own account had been summarily executed, but once the generals were called into council and became locked in their own disputes, all attempts to organize an orderly and equitable way of dividing the spoils broke down and each contingent of troops sent out its scavengers in packs. Requisitioning carts and pack-animals wherever they could find them, they loaded them with golden effigies, silver cauldrons, copper ingots, tripods, ewers, dishes, rhytons, chalices, torques, pectorals, jewelled diadems, rich tapestries and drapes, anything of value that could be moved. Arguments broke out over the choicer items of spoil. Old rivalries turned vicious with greed. Blood was shed. Meanwhile the gale that had got up across the Phrygian plain began to blow harder and men were injured in the drive to load herds of stolen cattle and horses onto ships that dipped and lurched in the choppy waters of the bay.

By late morning of the first day after the fall of the city,

Agamemnon was in a filthy temper. He hadn't slept for two nights. He was exhausted from the effort of trying to control his rampaging troops. Wine had left him with a thunderous headache, and now he seemed doomed to listen to interminable wrangling in the council about how a fair division of the spoils could be achieved. Not for the first time he found himself missing the cool, discriminating mind of Palamedes. The young Euboean had applied himself to this very problem after the fall of Smyrna and had come up with a solution; but his system had been so complicated that no one could remember quite how it worked, and now he was dead. Nor, with the possible exception of the still-absent Odysseus, was there anyone else who commanded sufficient respect to act as arbiter. So the arguing went on.

Meanwhile Agamemnon had things on his mind which he had not yet shared with his squabbling council. Prominent among them were thoughts of Cassandra as he had seen her, several hours earlier, in the temple of Athena. She stood, grasping the Palladium in her slender arms for protection while Locrian Aias lifted her shift from behind to reveal her naked flesh. Agamemnon had entered the temple in time to prevent the rape but the image was seared on his mind. And he had spoken to Cassandra. He had seen her breasts through the torn shift and looked into her face and found himself beguiled by the wild, penetrating gaze with which her eyes defied him. It was like being looked at by a wounded lynx.

Driven by an impulse of desire, Agamemnon had turned to his herald Talthybius, ordering that Cassandra be kept aside as part of his own portion in the spoils. As swiftly, as unconsciously, as that, the thing had been done.

And he wanted her now. He wanted her very badly, but he must sit here in this half-wrecked throne-room, listening to Acamas complain that there could be no justice if those who had fought throughout all ten years of the war were to see no more profit from their pains than those, such as the stripling Neoptolemus, who had only recently arrived.

Then Demophon, who had slipped earlier in a pool of blood and cracked his forehead, was declaring that as this relative newcomer had already seized Polyxena for his own purposes, should the others not be offered adequate compensation from his share for her removal from the lottery?

Neoptolemus, of course, would hear not a word of this. Why should a man be penalised for piously avenging his father's murder? No personal gain had accrued to him from Polyxena's death. Lesser men should be grateful that their own names would live for ever in the reflected glory of Achilles' fame rather than seeking to defraud the hero's son of a portion of his just reward.

Agamemnon groaned as the argument went on. Rueing the day that Odysseus had persuaded him to have Palamedes stoned, he was wondering where the Ithacan had got to now that his advice was needed. 'Let us at least agree to the division of the women!' he shouted. 'I have taken Cassandra for myself. Does anyone question that?'

Far from questioning it, most of the council were as relieved by their leader's eccentric choice as they were astonished by it. Who else would want a mad girl prowling round his house? So Agamemnon reclined back on Priam's throne, drumming his fingers with satisfaction. 'Let lots be drawn for Andromache then.'

Again Neoptolemus stepped forward. 'I have a prior claim to Hector's wife. Why should I trust her to chance?'

'How so?' Old Nestor wearily demanded. Still grieving for the death of his son Antilochus in a brutal skirmish only days before the war ended, the King of Pylos had taken little pleasure in the victory. This undignified squabbling appalled him.

'Andromache is mine on two counts,' the young warrior declared. 'Firstly, because she fell to me at the sacking of the city. She is the captive of my spear. But she is also mine by right of inheritance from my father who slew her husband in fair fight. Had Achilles lived he would certainly have claimed her for his own. I claim the wife of Hector in his name.'

'But your father's dead,' Acamas protested, 'and you've already claimed Polyxena in his name.'

His brother Demophon turned his bandaged head to the rest of the council. 'Does this boy mean to have all the women for himself?'

Neoptolemus bristled. 'Polyxena was offered in sacrifice to my father's shade.'

'You had your choice,' Demophon came back. 'The sword wasn't the only weapon you might have stuck her with. Or were you afraid the other wasn't yet keen enough.'

'Silence!' Agamemnon roared as he saw Neoptolemus' hand move towards his sword. 'Haven't we spilled enough Trojan blood that we must fight each other now?' When the murmurings in the hall had died down round him, he said, 'There are women enough to go round. And the treasure we have taken will make all of you rich for life. So be patient and let's try to sort this thing in an orderly manner.'

'But if we are to argue the claims of the dead as well as those of the living,' Acamas protested, 'the women will all be as old as Hecuba before we're done.'

'In any case,' Diomedes put in, 'this division cannot fairly take place until Menelaus and Odysseus are here to guard their interests.'

'Then let them be found at once,' Agamemnon growled. 'We cannot haggle like this for ever.'

He gestured to Talthybius who was about to leave the throne-room when Menelaus strode through the space where the two great gold-plated doors had already been removed from their hinges. Unlike any of the other men assembled there he had found time to bathe and change out of his battle-gear and looked so spruce in the looted vermilion robe he wore that his appearance stunned his grimy comrades to silence.

'So you've decided to show your face at last,' Agamemnon said. 'It looks as though you've been relaxing at the barbers while some of us were fighting a war.'

'The war is over, brother,' Menelaus answered. 'We have prevailed. I see no reason why one should not behave like a civilized man again.' But there was less confidence in his voice than in the defiant gaze he cast over the other lords.

Agamemnon studied him in disbelief. 'Can we presume,' he returned, 'that your business is concluded and your faithless wife is dead?'

'She is under close confinement. Deiphobus, however, is despatched.'

Narrowing his gaze, Agamemnon was about to say more but then decided it would be wiser to pursue this matter in private. His intentions were forestalled, however, by Demophon who asked eagerly, 'Does this mean that Helen will be included in the lottery along with the other captive women?'

The question was addressed not to Menelaus but to Agamemnon, who scowled at his brother, saying, 'I'm not sure what it means.'

Seeing his difficulty, Nestor intervened. 'You are speaking of the former Queen of Sparta,' he said sharply to Demophon. 'Her fate is surely for her husband, the King, to decide?'

Once more everyone looked to Menelaus, who had blanched at the exchanges.

The hall fell silent round him. The noise of men loading wagons ready for delivery to the ships could be heard from the courtyard. Somewhere an ass brayed under a beating from a stick.

'Well?' said Agamemnon.

'Helen's fate is not yet decided.' When the silence in the room sharpened to a new pitch of dissatisfaction, Menelaus saw that more was required. 'I am considering taking her back to Sparta and handing her over to those who have lost their loved ones in this war. I doubt she will last long in their hands.' Sensing that most of the men assembled in the hall would prefer either to witness Helen's death immediately or enjoy the pleasures of her body at leisure, he looked up with a pugnacious jut to his chin. 'But this much I promise you: my wife will never stand like a harlot in the public street for men to haggle over.'

'So if she lives you keep her?' Diomedes said.

'I know you've lusted over her for years,' Menelaus snapped back at him. 'But believe me, Diomedes, she'll never be yours. Nor shall any other man here lay hands on her.'

A general muttering broke out among the members of the council, above which rose the angry voice of Demophon. 'So, Agamemnon has already taken Cassandra for himself. Neoptolemus has killed Polyxena and lays claim to Andromache. Now Menelaus tells us that Helen will be withheld from the lottery. That leaves precious few of the royal women left for the rest of us, except that raddled hag Hecuba, of course, and who in his right mind would choose to be saddled with her?'

'I will take Hecuba.'

The voice had come from the back of the throne room near where the gold-plated double doors once stood. Everyone turned to see who had spoken.

It was Odysseus, who had just come from two painful encounters, both of which had further shaken his already troubled mind.

The most recent was with Antenor who had accosted him outside the palace and told him how he had been thrown down the palace steps by guards who were under orders not to admit him into Agamemnon's presence.

'Have you neither shame nor honour, Odysseus of Ithaca?' he shouted, white-faced and trembling. 'You swore to me that all Trojan citizens who laid down their arms would be spared, yet there is scarcely a man left alive in this whole city. You swore it to me and are now forsworn before the gods themselves. They know you for a fouler villain in this evil than even that foul brute in there.'

Odysseus held out a hand to steady the desperate old man, but Antenor spurned him as if contaminated by the touch.

Knowing that his words could make no difference, Odysseus said, 'Believe me, this was never my intention.'

'You gave me Agamemnon's word. You swore you spoke with his full authority.'

'I believed that I did. I truly believed it. But it seems I was deceived.'

'You're asking me to believe that he lied to you as you have lied to me? Why should I believe a word that any of you say? And what difference can it make? The dead are still dead whether you desired it or not. There is no mending that. And I curse you, Odysseus of Ithaca, for the fool's part you made me play in it.'

'We are both Agamemnon's fools,' Odysseus said, 'and both his victims too, though the gods know my suffering is as nothing compared with yours. Come inside with me, Antenor. Let us face him together.'

'He won't see me.' Antenor shook his white head. 'I've been demanding to speak with him since I came out of my house and saw . . . this.' He gestured hopelessly towards a pile of corpses. 'But he won't answer to me. His guards have kept me from the palace. Look.' He raised his robe to show where his pathetically thin shins were barked and bloody.

'We shall go in together, friend,' Odysseus urged him. 'They won't refuse you entry if you are at my side.'

But he was wrong. An armed troop of Agamemnon's Mycenaean Guard stood at the entrance to the palace and though they acknowledged Odysseus with a respectful salute, their commander was resolute that Antenor should not pass. 'The High King has more urgent matters on his mind,' he said. 'He will deal with this fellow in good time.'

'Without this fellow's help,' Odysseus protested, 'we could never have entered Troy. He is king here now and deserves your respect. Now let us through.'

'There is only one king here that I know of,' the commander answered, 'and he gives me my orders. I know he's been expecting you for some time, sir. But if this Trojan values his life he would do well to keep out of the High King's sight.'

Angry and humiliated, Odysseus was left with no choice but

to enter the palace alone. Having forced his way through the crowded vestibule, he stood in disbelief for some time, fingering his beard as he listened to the ill-tempered wrangling in the throne-room. A single glance at the flushed face and bleary eyes told him that Agamemnon was drunk, but he was amazed at the contrast between the dapper figure now cut by Menelaus and the dishevelled wreck of a man he had seen in Helen's bedroom. Everyone else in the hall had been so intent on the discussion of Helen's fate that his own arrival passed unnoticed. But now he had spoken and Agamemnon turned a scowl his way, demanding to know where he had been hiding himself.

Odysseus moved forward to stand before the King. 'I've been taking the measure of our achievement here,' he answered steadily.

Agamemnon chose to ignore the note of sarcasm in the Ithacan's voice. 'Well, there's one thing on which we're all agreed: that thanks to your guile we've just won what is probably the greatest victory of all time.'

'It will certainly rank among the greatest crimes.'

As others gasped around him, Odysseus held Agamemnon in his cold gaze. 'Last night you had the chance to become a truly great king. You already rule all Argos and might have ruled half of Asia out of Troy. Instead you seem content to be thought a brigand and a liar. You have betrayed your own honour and defiled mine. I find it small wonder that you can't look Antenor in the face.'

Momentarily shaken by the accusations, Agamemnon glanced away. Then he glowered back at his accuser. 'Let Antenor go home and count himself lucky he had the sense to betray his king rather than die with him.' Before Odysseus could utter a retort, he raised a menacing hand and struck back at the insult he had been offered. 'Nor should you trouble me with your cheap talk of honour. I heard none of that when you urged the death of Palamedes on me.'

'Palamedes was a traitor.'

'So you say. So you say.' Agamemnon narrowed his eyes in a

dangerous squint. 'In any case, what is your Trojan friend Antenor if not a traitor? Beware, Odysseus, lest you become one too.'

Around them, the silence of the hall intensified. The two men glared at one another. Odysseus was about to speak again when Menelaus stepped forward to forestall him, declaring out loud to the whole company that no one doubted the honour of Odysseus or his loyalty to the cause. He turned to smile uneasily at the glowering Ithacan. 'This is our hour of triumph, Odysseus. Rejoice in it.'

'No sane man rejoices over a massacre,' Odysseus replied. 'My heart quails at what we've done in this place.' He glowered back at Agamemnon. 'You wanted to know what I've been doing? I've just come from Queen Hecuba who threw herself at my knees and told me something I didn't know till now: that it was she who interceded with King Priam to spare my life. Yes and your life too, Menelaus, when we came as ambassadors into Troy. If it had not been for her and Hector, speaking up in our defence, Deiphobus would have murdered us in our beds that night. And now Hecuba was beseeching me to save the life of her daughter Polyxena. But I had to tell her that her plea came too late. I had to tell her that Polyxena was already dead. She died because Neoptolemus wanted her dead and because King Agamemnon assented to her death. And she died bravely with her breast bared under the sword because she *wanted* to die rather than endure any more of the suffering we have inflicted on her people. So I had no comfort for that wretched queen, and she had only curses for me and for the entire Argive host.' By now Odysseus was shaking as he spoke. 'It was from those curses that I learned how Locrian Aias tried to rape Cassandra in the temple of Athena. Of *Athena*, I say – the very goddess who came to me in a dream and gave us victory. Yet we have defiled her holy place with our lust and taken her sacred image as spoil. And this on top of the slaughter of countless men who lay down their arms because they saw no hope except in our mercy. *And all of this in breach of our given word.*'

Out of the silence someone jeered, 'You did your share of the killing, Odysseus. I saw you going at it like a man possessed.'

Odysseus turned and held the man's stare. 'To my shame I acknowledge it. But I for one take no pride in such a victory. I accept my share in guilt. And I will be amazed if the gods fail to punish us for the crimes we have committed here.'

'Enough,' Agamemnon bellowed. 'Would you call down the wrath of the gods on all our heads?'

When Odysseus answered grimly that he feared that was done long before he spoke, Agamemnon leapt to his feet. 'I've heard enough of this. Keep your shame to yourself, Odysseus of Ithaca. War is war and men fight and win it as best they can. We have done nothing that Priam and his Trojans would not have done to us had the gods given them the chance. Nothing, do you hear me? Now this council is over. I'll summon it again when you're all back in your right minds.'

Throwing his cloak over his shoulder, the King of Men commanded Menelaus to follow him and strode from the throne-room with an angry din of dissension breaking at his back.

The Strength of Poseidon

Menelaus, meanwhile, was also in trouble with his conscience. Always aware that his brother's ambitions had extended as far as Troy even before Paris came to Sparta, he still cherished the belief that the war was fought principally on his own behalf. Hadn't all Argos rallied to help him regain his lost honour? Yet here, at the end, when the city had finally fallen to the cunning of Odysseus and the onslaught of the Argive host, he had played almost no part in the triumph.

True, he had been among the band who risked those dangerous hours riding inside the wooden horse. True, he had personally killed Deiphobus who was the leader of the Trojan forces in all but name. But since that convulsion of fury in the bedroom of Helen's mansion, he had done nothing. Least of all had he been able to bring himself to kill his faithless wife, for where Helen was concerned, his spirit had succumbed to a stultifying lethargy so debilitating that he believed some god must be present between them in that chamber, forbidding her to flee and him to act. But how to convince anyone else of this, particularly his own brother, who sat scowling across from him now in the state-room where Priam had kept his father's charred throne as a reminder of the disaster that had once befallen Troy?

'You see what has begun to happen?' Agamemnon said, throwing his weight down on that throne. 'No sooner have they triumphed over the common enemy than they begin to fight amongst themselves. And Odysseus openly insults me. I tell you it's going to be harder asserting my authority now than it was before the walls were breached.' Then he raised his voice in a menacing growl. 'And what kind of example does my own brother set? Where were you during all those hours when I could have used you at my side? And why in the name of all the gods does that faithless Spartan bitch still live?'

'Need I remind you,' Menelaus said quietly, 'that my wife is your wife's sister?'

'You still think of her as your wife, do you, after she's dragged the good name of the House of Atreus through all the dirt from Epirus to Egypt? Have you forgotten how she cuckolded you with that Trojan peacock Paris? Or how she had no more shame than to let Deiphobus paddle his fingers in her pool as soon as Paris was dead?' Agamemnon brought his fist down on the table. 'The whore is not fit to be spoken of in the same breath as her sister. But, believe me. if Clytaemnestra had done to me what Helen has done to you, she wouldn't have lived a minute to tattle of it in the women's quarters. Have you no pride, man? Don't you care that you've become a laughing-stock out there, or that they're already laying bets on which of them will be the next to take his pleasure in Helen's bed if you're fool enough to let her live?'

During the years of the war Menelaus had lost much of the flowing head of red hair that had been his most striking feature. Flushed now under this withering assault from his brother's tongue, he passed a hand over his bald crown and down through the curls that remained above the nape of his neck. His eyes shifted around the painted chamber which still smelled of the pungent incense that King Priam had recently burned. He saw the Hours and Graces dancing there among the asphodels and the world seemed to sway around him like a sickly dream. He was biting his bottom lip hard enough to make it bleed.

And things were never meant to be like this. He had always imagined that once he was inside Troy he would swoop to his vengeance like an angry god. Yet he had brought the largest army that men had ever seen half-way across the world to seize his faithless wife, and thousands of men had died in the struggle, and still he dithered.

He was filled, in those moments, with a violent hatred for his brother. Yet he knew that Agamemnon spoke the truth. After Helen had so egregiously betrayed him, he could not take her back into his bed without making himself ridiculous before the hard-bitten men who had risked everything to help him to his vengeance. The humiliation he was suffering now would be multiplied a thousandfold when others, unconstrained by brotherly pride, began to smirk and jest behind their hands.

'The only question,' he conceded gruffly, 'is whether she dies here in Troy or at home in Sparta where her shame will be greater.'

Agamemnon shook his head. 'The only question is why she isn't dead already. Can't you see it? The longer she lives the more dissension her beauty will cause. We already know it has the power to make men mad.'

And here again, Menelaus saw it at once, his brother was in the right of it.

The power of that beauty had arrested his own sword-hand in the very moment when he had the chance to extinguish it for ever. Only here, away from her, beyond the reach of her allure, could he see how the glamorous enchantment worked and why he had been unmanned by it. Just to look at her again had been like sipping on a drug that paralysed his will.

But now his head was clear. Everything was clear to him again. Helen must die. She must die in a public place before the entire Argive host. Like a man waking from a bewildering dream he wondered how he could not have seen it sooner. Helen must die. And she must die by his own hand. His manhood depended on her death. The honour of the House of Atreus depended on it.

Helen's beauty had already dragged the world into a war longer and more terrible than any that mortal men had endured before: it must not be allowed to do so again.

'Yes,' he said as if speaking to himself, 'she has to die.'

Agamemnon's thoughts were already drifting elsewhere. He was thinking about Cassandra and the peculiar allure she exercised on his own senses. Too much of the day had already been wasted wrangling with words.

Impatiently he looked back at his brother. 'You will attend to it then?'

Menelaus swallowed, and nodded his head.

'Today?'

'Not today.' Menelaus withstood his brother's irascible glare. 'I want them all to witness it . . . the whole host. But they're looting the city still. I think she should be executed in a public ceremony . . . just before we take to the ships.'

Agamemnon considered the proposal for a moment. Such a last vivid memory of Troy would send the host of Argos back home with the knowledge that the honour of his house had not gone unredeemed. It would leave no one in doubt that the sons of Atreus accomplished what they set out to do. 'Very well!' he nodded. 'But you must let the captains know what you intend. Tell them at once and put an end to their fantasies. And make sure that Helen is kept under close guard. I don't want her wheedling her way round any of them. Now leave me. I have other things on my mind.'

But the Lion of Mycenae was not yet to be allowed the freedom of his desires, for Talthybius was waiting in the doorway as Menelaus went out, and there was a troubled frown on the herald's face.

'What is it now?' Agamemnon growled.

'Not good news,' Talthybius said. 'A ship has just put in from Iolcus. It was sent urgently by Peleus nearly a week ago. There's been an invasion into Magnesia from the north. A siege was closing round Iolcus when the ship put out. Its captain fears that the city may already have fallen.'

'Am I to be allowed no peace?' Agamemnon roared. 'Let Peleus look to his own troubles. I have problems enough here.' He got up and crossed to a window where he looked down on a gang of men who were struggling to lift the golden statue of Phrygian Aphrodite they had dropped while loading it into the back of an ox-cart. One arm had snapped off in the fall. The lovely thing was ruined and would have to be melted down.

Talthybius coughed discreetly. 'Need I remind my lord that Peleus sent almost his entire force of Myrmidons to our aid.'

Agamemnon turned to frown at him. 'What's been happening back there?'

'The situation isn't entirely clear but there are rumours that the sons of Acastus have joined forces with the Dorians and are out to wrench back Magnesia from Peleus's control.'

'Acastus? Who's he? I don't remember him.'

'Old Nestor is the only one left who knew him. He was king in Iolcus once but he's been dead for many years. He and Peleus were friends when they were young, but then his crazy wife falsely accused Peleus of trying to rape her when he spurned her advances. Acastus tried to have Peleus put to death but failed. Then he was killed himself when Peleus advanced an army out of Thessaly to settle his score. Peleus seized the whole kingdom of Magnesia at that time.'

'This is all ancient history,' Agamemnon snapped impatiently. 'What has any of it to do with me?'

'Perhaps a great deal,' Talthybius answered. 'With the Myrmidons fighting over here for us, Magnesia was left wide open to attack from a well-organized force. No such force was threatening Iolcus when we left, of course, but it seems that while we've been busy here in Troy, the Dorians have gathered their strength west of the Axius River and now they've moved south. They're ferocious fighters . . . and there's something else.' Talthybius hesitated, worried by what he had to tell. 'There's talk that some of them carry weapons made of a magical new metal. One that is much harder than bronze.'

The herald saw the creases deepen on the High King's brow. Agamemnon said, 'What else do we know about them?'

'Not much, except that they're barbarians. Until now they've stayed far enough to the north not to bother us. But it seems the world's been changing in the last ten years. We'd scarcely heard of the Dorians before we left for Troy and now look where they are. I can't imagine they care much about the sons of Acastus but they'll be happy enough to use them as figureheads. And once they've secured a foothold in Iolcus, they'll be poised to advance further south.'

'Unless they're stopped,' Agamemnon sighed, beating his fist against the arm of the throne as though hammering a nail into the blackened wood.

'Yes,' Talthybius nodded, 'unless they're stopped.'

'And Peleus can't hold them?'

'Not without the Myrmidons.'

'And he's an old man, long past his best.' Agamemnon narrowed his eyes. 'Do Neoptolemus and Phoenix know about this yet?'

'They're in council with Philoctetes right now. His citadel at Meliboea is also under threat. I doubt they'll be with us much longer.'

Agamemnon nodded, thinking quickly. It seemed that enemies were like the fabled dragon's teeth: you dealt with one only to see others spring up in your face. He said, 'It could have happened at a worse time, I suppose. Troy is ours now and I've no further need of the Myrmidons here. In fact, they'll be more use to me holding off these Dorians than arguing over plunder with the rest of the host. And I shan't be sorry to see the back of Neoptolemus. He's almost as dangerous as his father and less predictable. The sooner we're rid of him the better.' He looked up at his herald, frowning. 'A magical new metal, you say?'

'Their smiths smelt it from some ore they dig out of the earth. The rumour is that bronze swords break against it.'

Agamemnon shrugged uneasily. 'Well, a man's strength and courage count for more than the weapons he wields. And warriors don't come any tougher than the Myrmidons.' He gave a little, scoffing laugh. 'Let them and the Dorians slug it out across Thessaly together while we look to our own interests in the south.'

'There is still a difficulty,' Talthybius said, and glanced away when Agamemnon glowered at him. 'The question of Andromache remains unsettled. Neoptolemus still lays claim to her.'

Agamemnon scowled. Was there no end to the demands on him? His first impatient thought was that he had no personal interest in the woman's fate. Then a further thought occurred to him. 'I don't want that argument opened up again,' he decided. 'If we put Andromache to the lots then sooner or later someone will question my right to take Cassandra without doing the same. Let the boy take her – and much pleasure may she give him!'

Talthybius pursed his lips. 'It will cause trouble. Acamas and Demophon already feel they are being treated unjustly. They are not alone in this.'

'Then if they want Hector's wife so badly let them chase Neoptolemus across the Aegean for her. Tell him to stow her below decks and put to sea at once.'

'But . . .'

'I shall deny I knew anything about it when he's gone, of course.' Agamemnon smirked at his herald. 'In any case, they'll forget about women once they start counting out gold. Now have Cassandra brought to me, and get me some wine.'

Alone among the Trojan women Cassandra was not devastated by grief. On the contrary, a hectic elation had possessed her spirit almost from the moment when she heard the invading army enter Troy. Such further evidence of madness appalled her mother, for Hecuba had no understanding of how the catastrophic events of the night had brought, for this, the strangest, least congenial of her daughters, a final vindication of her long derided powers of prophetic insight.

Even while she had stood clutching the ancient woodwork of the Palladium, with the breath of Aias hot on her neck and his hands tearing at her shift and his gang of spearmen coarsely egging him on, Cassandra knew herself as safe in the possession of the goddess as if she had been surrounded by a ring of astral fire. So it had been no surprise to her when Agamemnon strode into that violated sanctuary, saw the unholy thing that was happening there and immediately put a stop to it. What astonished her, however, was the silent exchange of sensual energy that took place between herself and the Lion of Mycenae as they stared into each other's eyes.

She had expected to be filled with hatred for the man. She had willed all the venom she could muster into her voice when she hissed out her brief answers to his questions. And this show of implacable hostility was the only thing evident to those around them. But for the two of them the deep truth of the encounter was quite different. They were like souls disturbingly familiar to each other from another time, another country – another life even – come together once more in a mutual shock of recognition. Yet where Agamemnon sensed only the tense, erotic charge in that meeting, Cassandra's deeper gaze flashed on a darker assignation lying in wait for them. She saw it so clearly that it frightened her. But then the goddess had spoken through the silence and the bewildered young woman understood that she alone was now invested with the power to wreak destruction on the House of Atreus. It was only a question of time.

None of the other captive women believed Cassandra when she tried to share her secret, just as no one had believed her when she warned of the doom that Paris must bring on Troy. But she was no longer demoralised by their disbelief. Already parts of the city were in flames. Soon, just as she had long prophesied, the whole of Troy would be reduced to a rubble of stones and smoking ash. And just as certainly Agamemnon would take her into his bed, utterly ignorant that in doing so he was embracing his own death. So Cassandra came to the king that afternoon with the serene docility of an animal consenting to the sacrifice.

For his own part, Agamemnon expected to see her cowering

before him, but the moment she entered the royal chamber, he knew himself in the presence of a powerfully composed young woman. Her eyes countered his appraising gaze as though it was he, not she, who had been summoned to this encounter. Smiling, she put her palms together, raised them to the delicate cleft of her chin and said, almost as if it was some conspiratorial joke between them, 'To think it has taken ten long years of war to bring us together!'

He uttered a gruff little snort of surprise. 'You think that's what it was all about? I understood it had something to do with my brother Menelaus and his wife's lust for your treacherous brother Paris.'

She smiled again. 'And with your desire for the wealth of Troy, of course.' She shrugged her narrow shoulders. 'But that is mere mortal fiddle. The gods have always had deeper intentions.'

Dryly he said, 'And they keep you informed of them?'

'They do.'

Agamemnon took a swig at his wine. 'Then you'd better come and sit down and tell me what they have in mind for us.'

'Union,' she said without moving. 'They mean to consecrate me as your bride.'

He stared at her in shock for a moment, and then, not knowing what else to do, he laughed.

'They mean for us to live together and die together,' she declared.

Uneasily he said, 'I already have a wife.'

Cassandra crossed the floor to stand before him. 'You have a queen,' she contradicted him, 'and your children have a mother. But I am the destined consort of your soul. It was for me you came to Troy.'

She reached out a finger to trace the contours of his face – the broad, bull-like brow, the scar at his temple, the craggy orbit of his eyes and cheekbone. He gasped a little as it came to a halt at his bearded chin. 'Can you deny,' she said, 'that you recognized it when we met in Athena's temple?'

Agamemnon could deny nothing. So closely was his heart knocking against his tonsils that he was, in fact, having some difficulty speaking at all. There remained a wary recess of his mind which suspected that he might be falling under some form of bewitchment, but the rest was vertiginously attracted to that condition.

In so far as wounds and an excess of wine permitted it, Agamemnon had taken brief pleasure throughout the years of the war with a constantly changing harem of concubines and slave-girls. Most of them he could not remember, and in none had he met much more than an anxiety to please him that was bred only of fear and dread. But there remained, it seemed, an unanswered loneliness at the centre of his soul, and this woman had both divined and answered it. Here at last might be someone who recognized the man he truly was.

That had never been the case with Clytaemnestra. He had long since come to depend on his wife's shrewd intelligence and the skilful, pragmatic command she exercised over tedious details of finance and the subtler twists of court intrigue. But that was the only good in their marriage now. He had long since accepted that she would never for a moment worship him as he, when he was a shy youth exiled in Sparta, had once worshipped her. He had even learned to fear her severe, autocratic spirit, for though he had sired three children on her, he had never found any warmth in their marriage bed. There had always been too much which Clytaemnestra could never forget. And ever since the day he had put their daughter to death on the altar at Aulis, he had known that, whatever triumphal show the people of Mycenae might mount for him, his true eventual reception in that city would be far colder still.

Yet was it possible that for all the arid years he'd endured, and for all the bitterness still to come, there might just, in his hour of triumph, be a measure of consolation here?

A wary part of his mind could not quite bring itself to credit it.

Smiling, Cassandra whispered, 'I know what you're thinking. And I will answer your thought. Long ago I warned my father of what must happen if he took Paris back into his house, but he would not hear me. I warned him again when Helen came to Troy, and still he would not listen. So he brought destruction on himself, and though I spoke for the god, I could not prevent it. As for you, in destroying his house you are as much an instrument of the gods as I am.' Smiling, she added, 'We are not to blame, Agamemnon, if our true power goes unrecognized.'

Standing gravely before him, Cassandra removed two ivory combs and shook loose the piled tresses of her hair. Then she crossed her hands at her shoulders and pulled down her gown along slender arms.

Breathless, lips slightly agape, Agamemnon stared in wonder at her small bared breasts. He saw the nipples appear, dark almost as figs against unblemished flesh. 'Come,' she said and reached out an inviting hand. Then the King of Men was suckling gratefully at her bosom like a hungry child.

Helen, meanwhile, remained a prisoner in the city where she had always been a prisoner. Even in the days when Paris was alive and the two of them were still lost in their dream of love, she had never felt free to roam the streets of Troy or venture alone into the wooded hills beyond the plain of the Scamander as she had done in Sparta when she was a girl. Too many Trojans envied and resented her, so Paris was reluctant to let her stray far from his sight. And then the Argive host had come, and her enemies inside the city found larger cause to hate her. Helen had felt herself besieged inside a city under siege, and now that city had fallen and she was merely one among a throng of captive women, but kept apart from the others for fear they might vent their despair on the beauty that had brought them so much grief. And she lacked a single friend to comfort her, for even her old bondswoman Aethra, the mother of Theseus, had been joyfully released by her grandsons Acamas and Demophon, and would soon be on her way home to pass her dying years at home in Troizen or Athens.

Because the mutilated body of Deiphobus still lay in the chamber she had shared with him, Helen sat alone in the smaller room where Aethra had slept.

She had found in the bondswoman's care the nearest thing she had known to a mother's love since she had been a very small child, and she imagined that some vestige of that security might still be found among the things that belonged to her. But without Aethra's presence the things were only things, and for many hours Helen had been terrified by the knowledge that, for her, there was no security anywhere in this devastated city.

She had tried to prepare herself for death but she had no talent for philosophy and there was no comfort to be found in prayer. It seemed that her father Zeus had turned his face from her, and to which of the goddesses could she pray with any hope of being heard? Aphrodite, on whose altar she had thrown away her life, had failed her already. Hera would not countenance the violation of the marriage bond, and Divine Athena, whose votive horse looked down across the city, had brought destruction on Troy and all who dwelt there. There remained Artemis, the goddess Helen had revered as a girl, but Artemis had not saved her all those years ago when Theseus abducted her from the woodland shrine. Nor had that goddess spurned the offering when the innocent Iphigenaia was put to her father's knife on the altar in Aulis. There was, it seemed, no pity there.

There was no pity anywhere.

Outside she could hear men shouting as they plundered the house that had once belonged to Hector and Andromache. Somewhere a hungry baby cried. Black smoke gusted on the wind that rattled the shutters and agitated the trees. The whole world was in turmoil and she sat at the centre of it, isolated and afraid.

Soon it would be dark and with the darkness Menelaus would return and both her greatest fears and her only hope were fixed on that moment. If she could prevail on him to spare her again, then she might survive the fall of Troy. But if, as she suspected, Agamemnon were to bully his brother with primitive talk of honour and revenge, then she would never leave this room alive.

And there was no saying which way things would go, for when the world was turned upside down, all things were prey to the random chance of war.

How to better her own chances then?

Should she remain like this, unkempt and bedraggled by weeping, and thus make a last appeal to whatever reserves of pity might be left to Menelaus? Or should she brush out her hair, put on a gown that enhanced the light in her eyes, coax the colour back into her cheeks, and present herself to his senses as the woman he had always adored?

Either choice might work. Either could prove disastrous. She was incapable of decision. Then she remembered that what had stayed his sword in the moment when he might have killed her was the sight of the breasts she had instinctively bared. The beauty which had always been her curse had become her salvation. Perhaps it might save her again.

She had been sitting at her dressing table for only a few moments and was tying back her hair before applying the paint to her face when the door of the room banged open and Menelaus was standing there. She could detect no hint of mercy in his baleful stare.

He took in the signs of weeping round her blotchy eyes. He saw how pale and distraught her face. He saw that the hands she lowered from the nape of her neck were trembling. Menelaus felt an answering faintness at the back of his knees when she sighed like a woman renouncing all hope and said, 'You have come to tell me I must die.'

'Yes.'

'Is it to be now?'

'No, not yet. But tomorrow. You should prepare yourself.'

Her throat was dry, her smile wan as she said, 'And how am I to do that?'

He glanced away from the beseeching reach of her gaze. 'As best you can,' he said tersely, and left the room before she could unman him once more.

With the naked bulk of Agamemnon's body sleeping beside her, Cassandra lay awake far into the night, elated by the knowledge that at last she was coming into the fullness of her powers. This grim man, the Lion of Mycenae, High King of all the Argives, enemy and destroyer of Troy, was as pliable in her hands as clay.

Before he slumped into sleep, she had lain placidly on her parents' great bed while he nuzzled at her breasts and kissed the soles of her feet, abasing himself before her body. Earlier, she had watched him mount to the climax of his passion like a man battering at the gate of a city that he believed he would never take; and when – already chafed by the force of his thrusts – she saw how his frustration must soon turn to rage, she whispered a spell in his ear that might have come to her from a god. His eyes had widened. The grim set of his mouth eased into a gasp, and he was crying out in gratitude as he released all the tension of his body into her unresisting warmth.

As for herself, the only pleasure Cassandra took from the act resided in the knowledge that strength was being purchased by her pain. And the shedding of her virgin blood had been a kind of investiture. Already she had known that sexual congress was charged with magical power, but now she had felt that power rising within her at every thrust, and in the moment when Agamemnon shuddered his seed into her loins, a net had been thrown over him that was as fine and inescapable as the net in which Hephaestus once trapped Aphrodite and her lover Ares. Utterly unaware of what was happening, the King of Men lay gasping in its trammels like a landed fish.

Again Cassandra smiled to think how the spell which he had taken for the key to his release had been, in truth, a binding spell. Agamemnon was hers now. He was hers as she would never be his.

Smoke and moonlight drifted through the window casement. The still night breathed about her head. Troy, the capital city of death, was filled with sleepers and the dead. For much of that night only Cassandra lay fully awake, gazing down the galleries of time to where her final consummation waited: Agamemnon dead; the House of Atreus deeper mired in its heritage of blood; the city of Mycenae reduced in turn to ruin. Far-sighted Apollo might have rejected her all those years ago so that no one would believe her when she spoke. But soon, quite soon, every one of her prophesies would be fulfilled.

Cassandra was smiling as she entered sleep.

Towards dawn, she jumped awake, her head dizzy with a pain that felt both sickly and thunderous. Agamemnon still snored, untroubled, at her side. The drapes at the casement were blowing in the wind and a jagged light, the colour of sulphur, stained the darkness of the sky outside. Whether it came from the moon or a pallid sun she could not say, for it had a drastic, raw sheen she associated with neither. Her nose distinguished the mingled smells of burning and decay. Every cell of her body started to quiver with alarm.

Then the sound rose round her, a sound such as she had never heard before. She imagined the muffled groans of an imprisoned titan locked inside the earth; but then it broke louder on her ears, a harsh grinding as of monstrous millstones disrupted in their toil. Dust fell in a fine powdery shower on her face. The bed was shaking. The walls seemed to stagger before her gaze. Cassandra leapt from the bed and found the floor moving beneath her feet.

Agamemnon sat up clutching at the blankets as the bed-frame juddered round him. He was shouting like a drunken man woken from a dream. 'What is it? What is it?' But his voice was buried under the groan of the quaking earth.

The noise increased in volume, shuddering through her flesh, blurring her vision, hurting her ears. She winced at the panicked rattling of shutters, the creak and jarring of the beams. As though it was about to faint, the palace swayed.

Then it stood still again. The dawn air held its breath.

After several seconds she heard voices shouting in the street outside. A cloud of dust gusted across the room. Agamemnon jumped naked from the bed. 'We should get out of here. The shock may come again.'

Cassandra turned to him and smiled. 'That was Poseidon warning of his strength,' she said quietly. 'But calm yourself. It's not yet our time to die.'

An Audience with the Queen

Unaware of the stratagem of the wooden horse and, therefore, that Troy was about to fall, Clytaemnestra stood on her balcony in the palace at Mycenae, gazing out across the olive groves and farms of the fertile valley at the foot of the crag. She was holding a wax tablet onto which her most trusted secretary had deciphered a message sent by one of her agents – a minister in the Hittite court whom she had suborned many years earlier when he first came to Mycenae as an imperial legate. The message informed her that Hattusilis, Emperor of the Hittites, had finally dealt with the unrest on his eastern border, and because he was unwilling to countenance a permanent Mycenaean presence in Troy, he was now considering committing the entire western division of the Hittite army to King Priam's aid.

And if that were to happen, Clytaemnestra thought as she gazed into the hazy light that hung like a veil across the bay of Argos, Agamemnon's expeditionary force was doomed.

Not quite a year had passed since she had taken her daughter Iphigenaia to Aulis, but her face had aged by much more than the months that had elapsed since then. These days Clytaemnestra slept so little and ate so little that her severe features were honed as spare as a windblown shell, and the vivid glitter of paint she applied around her eyes only accented the pallor of her skin. She might have been thought a decade older than her thirty-seven years.

The Queen of Mycenae had never been a woman to laugh easily or take pleasure in the trivialities of life, but not even her remaining children had seen her smile since she had returned from Aulis. More than ever, they were afraid of her.

Throughout the long night before Iphigenaia was put to death and during the day of the sacrificial ceremony itself, Clytaemnestra had been kept under guard in the fortress at Aulis. Had she possessed the strength, she would have struck her husband dead where he stood sooner than let him lay violent hands on her child. But this formidable queen, who had grown used to commanding the court of Mycenae in Agamemnon's absence and wielding all the instruments of civil power in his name, was now surrounded by forces with which she could not contend. Those forces were masculine and brutal and would baulk at nothing – not even the murder of a child – to impose their will on the world. And so, for all the power that had accrued to her, the Queen of Mycenae knew herself reduced to what she had always truly been – a woman in a world ruled by men. She was as helpless before their strength as a nymph ravished by a god.

Once the first frenzy passed and she realized that no one would answer her shouting and screaming and beating on the door, she had slumped into a trance of self-harm, tearing at her hair and dragging her nails along the flesh of her arms. Then she had resorted to prayer, but to which of the gods could a woman confidently pray when Artemis herself, the virgin goddess of unmarried girls and protector of the young, had demanded the life of her daughter as the blood-price of her husband's stupidity?

Both her daughter and her sister Helen had lavished their devotions on Artemis before all other gods, and what good had she brought to either of them? Helen had been abducted by Theseus even as she danced at the shrine of Artemis; and now, in only a few hours, Iphigenaia would lie dead across her altar.

And what of herself? Clytaemnestra had always given her first allegiance to Sky-Father Zeus, but she had fared no better. A long time ago Agamemnon had come to her in Elis and killed the husband she loved and commanded that her baby's brains be bashed out against a wall. Her prayers and imprecations had been of no more avail then than they were now at the imminent loss of this second child to the cruelty of men and gods. Her heart boiled with the pain of it.

She had finally fallen asleep out of sheer exhaustion, and in the small hours of the night a vision came to her.

In the vision she had strayed outside the city into the foothills of the mountains. She could hear birdsong and the clatter of wild water among stones. Her nostrils took in the smell of a damp green world. Unlike Helen, Clytaemnestra had never been at ease out in the wilds and she was trembling as she walked. Thorns scratched the skin of her calves. Gorse tore at the short tunic she wore. Flies droned about her ears. The sun lay heavy on her head. The whirr of crickets ratcheted to an unnerving pitch of intensity. When she looked up, black birds were wheeling above her in the glare. She sensed animals around her, inquisitive and hostile, aware of her as prey.

All her life Clytaemnestra had been a creature of the city. She was at home inside the busy world of court intrigue. Politics, diplomacy, commerce, trade relations, the intellectual traffic of art and cultural refinement, all such civil discourse was the very stuff of life to her. And because her chosen world began and ended inside city walls, she had taken little interest in the natural terrain beyond except in so far as it furnished the material necessities of life. Yet here she was, exiled from all things congenial and familiar, in a wilderness where the single law was that one devoured only to be, in turn, devoured.

Clytaemnestra began to run and the faster she ran the more afraid she became. Somewhere at her back a horn sounded. Her heart thudded against her ribs as the world swept past her in a dazed green swirl. She was sobbing as she ran and when she looked down she saw that her arms were covered with black bristles. There were bristles at her face and she was squinting out over a lengthening snout through which, like complicated music, passed a whole medley of scents. Then she was down on all fours, travelling quickly now, thrusting her dense bulk forward into the cover of the brakes.

For a moment she stood panting there, torn ears pricked, eyes peering at the light, hearing sour juices swill in the low-slung, churning cauldron of her belly. Then she caught the sharp, hot stink of hunting dogs. A pack of them howled and bayed behind her now. Clytaemnestra knew that she had been transformed into a boar, a wild sow, bristly, tusked and muscular, and she was now the single quarry of this forest-chase.

So she turned and ran again, scrambling among stones as she splashed her shoulders along a muddy water-course to scramble up a steep bank of scree. With the pack yelping and the hunter hallooing close behind her, and her breath no more than a hoarse, wheezing squeal, she burst through the thickets into the dim declivity of a cave she knew. Here she could turn and make her stand. Here she might hold the frantic pack at bay. But where she had expected to find a footing of solid rock, the soft earth sagged beneath her. Then she was falling, and turning as she fell, deeper and deeper into a vertiginous black pit where her bones must shatter when the falling stopped.

Clytaemnestra came to her senses in a place so dark and raw and ancient that it chilled her blood. She was alone except for a stone figure, only remotely human, that loomed above her. The charred bones of votive offerings lay scattered at its feet. There was, she knew at once, no exit from this place.

In a dim light emitted from the rock itself, Clytaemnestra looked up into the face of the Goddess. She found nothing radiant there, no virgin sheen, no curving silver bow. This was no maiden daughter of Zeus. She was far older than the Olympians, born of another primeval generation, an aboriginal survivor of the gods before the gods. A lion and a stag dangled helplessly in her grip.

Through hollows in her breasts protruded the sharp, rapacious curve of vultures' beaks.

Quailing, Clytaemnestra delivered herself over to an archaic power that was both the creator and the immolator of everything that dared to live. Her own face became a face of stone. Her tongue shrivelled to a stone. Her heart was stone and her ribs had turned to a cage of stone about it. She was the Queen of Stone in a place of stone. She could hear the hiss of snakes writhing about her feet. Her breasts had grown sharp as vulture's beaks.

By the time Clytaemnestra was released from confinement in Aulis, the contrary wind had turned, and the King of Men was sailing back to Troy with the blood of his daughter on his hands. His wife had not seen him since. Nor had she received any letters except those bringing instructions for the administration of the state he had left in her charge. She was secretly informed by her spy Talthybius that his master was drinking heavily and had a costive stomach; he was also short-tempered and slept badly. Otherwise the Lion of Mycenae was getting on with his war.

But as far as Agamemnon's dealings with his wife were concerned, the death of Iphigenaia was buried in a silence so deep the child might never have existed.

In the months since that vision had come to Clytaemnestra not a day passed without her renewing the cold strength that she derived from it. She drew on that strength as she placed the tablet on her desk and turned to confront the visitor who entered her chamber with a respectful bow of his gaunt head. King Nauplius of Euboea was more welcome in Mycenae than he could have guessed.

'It was good of your majesty to grant me a private audience so quickly,' he said. 'I know that the demands of state press heavily in the absence of your lord.'

'They do indeed,' she answered dryly, sitting at a large desk on which many papyrus scrolls and inscribed tablets were piled, 'so I beg you not to waste words preparing the ground, as I am quite sure you did with Penelope in Ithaca, and at the court of Diomedes in Tiryns, and in the House of the Axe on Crete.'

For some time before his arrival in Mycenae, Nauplius had been worrying about what course this encounter might take. Though his confrontation with Penelope had turned out badly, he had found Agialeia, the credulous young wife of Diomedes, entirely pliant to his will, and Queen Meda of Crete was already so voracious in her appetites that she had needed no encouragement to cuckold her absent husband Idomeneus. But Clytaemnestra was a more dangerous quarry. All Argos knew how much of Agamemnon's authority she had arrogated to herself. It would take a rash man to risk causing her offence and Nauplius had never been rash. But he was old and furious with grief and weary of life, and his single interest was in avenging the death of his son, for which satisfaction he was prepared to take whatever risks might be required.

Even so, as his litter was carried past the kingdom's great ancestral tombs, beneath the huge stone-built bastions, and on through the Lion Gate into the citadel, the shadows of Mycenae had closed down round him. Not having visited the city for many years, Nauplius had been impressed by its mighty show of power and wealth. The ramparts were formidable, of course, but the porphyry friezes and richly painted porticoes bespoke a vision of which that dull boor Agamemnon was surely incapable, and which must therefore be attributed to the ambition, taste and intelligence of his queen.

To come into her presence he had passed through a busy antechamber filled with ministers, legates and suppliants, all of whom were impatient to secure her attention once this audience was over, and then on through a warren of sentried passages. And those documents on her desk were not for show. Nauplius knew that her correspondence reached from Posidonia in the far west to the eastern kingdom of Mesopotamia, by way of the mighty

Hittite Empire and Pharaonic Egypt. And it was this woman whom he sought to make the instrument of his will.

Finding himself already outflanked in the first exchange, he masked his surprise with a wry smile. 'I see your majesty is well-informed. Does the mistress of the Lion House keep spies in place across all Argos?'

Clytaemnestra motioned for the old man to sit. 'Why should I need spies?' she shrugged. 'Your mission has been aimed at the wives of my husband's captains, and wives have a way of sharing secrets, especially where their husbands' misdemeanours are concerned.'

'Misdemeanours?' Still smiling, though with diminished confidence, Nauplius fingered the curls of his beard. 'You think of them so lightly.'

But Clytaemnestra merely appraised her visitor with faintly disdainful hauteur. 'I did not require my husband to swear a vow of celibacy when he took ship for war. He has his appetites. I expected him to sate them.' Having noted the unhealthy shadows round his eyes, she had already decided that there was not much time left in which to make use of this dying man.

Nauplius watched her reach for a wax tablet and glance at it as though already bored by this conversation. Having studied her negligent air for a moment, he said quietly, 'And did you also expect him to bring home an oriental concubine and make her his queen in Mycenae?'

Clytaemnestra lifted her gaze. 'I presume you can put a name to this rival for my throne?'

'Chryseis,' Nauplius answered at once.

'Chryseis?'

'A Trojan captive taken in the raid on Thebe, She is daughter to a priest of Apollo. Very beautiful, I understand. And also young.'

Clytaemnestra shook her head. 'But your news is old, Nauplius. Haven't you heard that Chryseis was returned to her father many weeks ago?' She uttered a further dismissive sigh and glanced back at the tablet, reading as she spoke. 'Not for the first time my husband offended a god. He was forced to surrender her in recompense. But I assure you he planned nothing more for the girl than a place among the many harlots who warm his bed.' Her painted eyes shifted back to the discountenanced King of Euboea. 'In some matters my husband is a fool, I acknowledge it freely; but women are of small importance to him. No, Nauplius. Your unsavoury gossip may have troubled the wives of Diomedes and Idomeneus, but I'm as little impressed by your lies as was my cousin Penelope.'

The corners of the old man's mouth drooped in an offended moue. Putting his weight on his staff, he made a show of getting to his feet. 'I came here in good faith. But if the Queen does not care to hear what I have to say . . .'

'Sit down,' Clytaemnestra interrupted him. 'You are not yet dismissed our presence.' She put the tablet down. 'You came here to make mischief. We both understand that. Let us not pretend otherwise.'

Nauplius narrowed his eyes. He might have overestimated this woman's readiness to hear him but he did not underestimate her power. His position was now fraught with danger. The palace was difficult to enter: it might prove far more difficult to leave, for this was Mycenae, a city as dark as it was golden, and there were guards at every door. Yet he thought he had detected something almost reassuringly conspiratorial in her last remark.

Thinking quickly, he said, 'I have a just grievance against your husband.'

'I have many,' she answered, 'though I find it wisest to keep them to myself.'

'I am speaking of the death of my son.'

'Palamedes was a traitor.'

'No more than I am myself,' Nauplius protested.

Clytaemnestra uttered a humourless, scoffing laugh. 'And this is loyalty?'

Nauplius clenched his fist at his knee. 'Agamemnon forfeited my allegiance when he commanded the wrongful death of my son.'

'If it was indeed wrongful.'

'My son was the innocent victim of slander and envy.'

'No one is innocent, Nauplius. In any case, it makes no difference.'

For a moment he thought everything lost. He too was about to be charged with treason. He too must brace himself to meet a traitor's death. But her eyes softened a little. A frown passed across her face like the outward sign of pain. 'Though there is no more grievous hurt,' she conceded, 'than the loss of a child.'

And quite suddenly he saw what this devious woman was about.

'Iphigenaia!' he whispered.

'Yes,' she hissed, 'Iphigenaia.'

'Then your majesty will understand the fury of my grief.'

'Oh I do, Nauplius. I understand it very well.'

'And wasn't there another child killed before her?' he risked. 'Long ago when you were queen in Elis.'

The green and gold paint around Clytaemnestra's eyes glittered in the light. When she looked up at him the hollows at her cheekbones seemed more deeply drawn. 'He was not yet six weeks old.' Her voice was almost without expression as she added, 'He too is among the many ghosts that haunt this place.'

By now Nauplius was contemplating possibilities that had been far from his mind when he set out for Mycenae. How absurd that he should have been worried about stirring up this woman's feelings against her husband when for so many years she had been cultivating her own patient hatred of the man.

As though complete understanding had now been established between them, he nodded in a show of sympathy. 'We have a common interest, it seems.'

But his presumption had been too eager. Her grief felt contaminated by proximity to his.

For what felt like a very long time Clytaemnestra studied the old king with distaste. In other circumstances, she might have been pleased to put a speedy end to his deceitful and vindictive life. But she had need of him now.

Mistaking the gist of her appraisal, a dreadful thought struck root in his mind. Surely she did not intend to appoint him as the immediate instrument of her vengeance? He was an old man, and sick. He was not the stuff of which assassins were made.

She let him sweat a moment longer before saying, 'You came here today with the intention of persuading me to betray my husband with some other man. Is that not so?' And when he glanced uncertainly away, 'That was your strategy with Penelope. You offered the same temptation to Queen Meda and Agialeia. Am I to understand you had a less attractive proposition to put to me?'

Uncertain of his ground once more, Nauplius replied evasively. 'Would you not agree that such humiliation is no less than a disloyal husband deserves?'

'And you would have been content with that? It would have satisfied you merely to see me cuckold the man you hold responsible for the death of your son? You disappoint me, Nauplius. I credited you with larger ambition.'

He was aware of her eyes taunting him to think the thoughts that she had put into his mind. But his breath was fetched short with anxiety and his face was grey. How to be sure she wasn't inciting him to condemn himself out of his own mouth? If she were to arraign him as a traitor, she would certainly be believed, as he would not should he seek to accuse her of complicity.

Again, without humour, she smiled. 'Are you afraid of me, Nauplius?'

'A man would be a fool,' he said, 'not to hold you in great respect.'

'Good,' she answered. 'Then we understand one another.' With a brisk, light touch, her fingers tapped the edge of the desk. Then she surprised him again with a change of direction. 'You know the whereabouts of Aegisthus, do you not?'

Nauplius looked up at her in amazement. Aegisthus had been on the run ever since his father, the usurper Thyestes, was toppled from the throne of Mycenae by Agamemnon's army many years ago. It was Aegisthus who, while still a small boy, had murdered

Atreus, the rightful king. Since Agamemnon had regained the Lion Throne, every attempt to find and kill his father's murderer, and thus put an end to a gruesome cycle of vengeance, had failed. How could Clytaemnestra know that Nauplius had made contact with him? What were her intentions now?

Irritated by the mute gape of the old man's mouth, Clytaemnestra tapped the desk with greater impatience.

Hoarsely, thinking quickly, Nauplius said, 'And if I did?'

'Then you might speak to him on my behalf.'

'And what would your majesty have me say?'

'Perhaps that the Queen of Mycenae does not look upon him with the same inveterate hatred as its king.'

Nauplius swallowed. 'I feel sure the heart of Aegisthus would be gladdened to hear this news.' His eyes shifted with his thoughts. 'But he has good cause to be wary,' he risked. 'How can he be sure of its truth?'

'Do you take me for a liar, Nauplius?'

'By no means. Yet Aegisthus will surely remember how his father Thyestes was once invited to return to Mycenae in what seemed a gesture of reconciliation . . . with what truly terrible consequences your majesty will certainly recall.'

Clytaemnestra's lips narrowed. The old man had dared to refer to an event that had been so horrifying in its impact on the imagination that no one in Mycenae had spoken of it for years. Yet even that silence seemed to taint the city's air.

Sharply Clytaemnestra said, 'That was in another time.'

Nauplius shrugged. 'But the shadows remain.'

'And will, as long as the House of Atreus rules in Mycenae.'

The implications of her statement astounded him. He knew he must be very careful now. In a voice as low as hers, for who could tell if these walls were recording every word, King Nauplius hissed, 'Does the Queen foresee a time when it may not?'

'Nothing lasts for ever.'

'Least of all a man's life.'

'Exactly so.'

'And for that reason Aegisthus will not put his own at risk unless he is given very strong assurances.'

Aware how momentous the step she was about to take, Clytaemnestra drew in her breath. 'Then let us be plain with one another. You may tell Aegisthus that if he has the stomach for it, I, and only I, can help him to regain what was once his father's throne here in Mycenae.'

Nauplius could feel his heart knocking at his ribs, but he merely nodded as though she had made no more than a further gambit in haggling over the price of some desirable commodity.

For the moment she offered nothing further, so his throat was dry as he said. 'If I were Aegisthus, might I not be wise to ask how I could be certain this was not some ruse devised by the High King's wife to lure her husband's most inveterate enemy out of hiding?'

Clytaemnestra nodded. 'Would an assurance sealed in blood satisfy him?'

'I would think,' Nauplius answered with a bleak smile, 'that would entirely depend on whose blood was shed.'

Having already anticipated every development of this wary conversation, Clytaemnestra nodded calmly. 'Even before my husband sailed to Troy, many of those in positions of power and influence in this court owed their good fortune entirely to my favour. There were others, of course, retainers of the House of Atreus from before my time, men to whom the High King feels a certain loyalty. Men he would not replace even though I urged him to do so. But ten years are a long time.' She lifted her eyes. 'There have been deaths, you understand.'

'As is only natural.'

'Yes. As is only natural. So there has been a need for new appointments.'

Nauplius recalled the intense young ministers and secretaries he had seen conferring in quick, low voices in the ante-room outside, every one of them no doubt loyal only to the formidable woman to whom they owed their preferment.

'However,' Clytaemnestra continued, 'a few remain who are not entirely under my control. There is one in particular. I am thinking of the court bard, Pelagon.'

'I know his reputation of old,' Nauplius said. 'I hear he is the greatest of singers.'

'So they say. The question is, for whom does he sing and on what theme?'

'You have found reason not to trust the bard?'

'He is Agamemnon's spy, left here in the court to keep me under surveillance. There are limits, you see, to the trust the High King places in his queen. It will not be long, therefore, before Agamemnon is informed of your visit to Mycenae. For that reason I shall, of course, inform him of it myself. Today, as soon as you are gone. I will write to him explaining why it was only because of your status as a royal guest of the house that I let you depart with your life.'

Nauplius held her dry stare for a time, thinking quickly ahead. 'But were your husband to learn that you were in communication with Aegisthus . . . ?'

'Precisely. Which is why he must never learn of it.'

'Then Pelagon must sing no more.'

'Neither must Agamemnon suspect his sudden silence.'

Nauplius considered this for a time. 'Does the bard ever leave Mycenae?'

'Pelagon is an old man with little interest in travel. But he is also vain and has a secret weakness for beautiful young men.'

'Then he might he be lured from the city by reports of such a person willing to grant him favours?'

'I think it more than possible.'

'Then I will speak with Aegisthus. Perhaps such a person could be found.'

Clytaemnestra narrowed her eyes. 'No shadow of suspicion can attend this matter. Whatever becomes of Pelagon, it must appear no more than an unhappy accident – though it would be well, I think, if it were to happen soon.'

'Aegisthus is a man of considerable resource.'

'I expected no less.'

'Indeed, I believe your majesty will find him an excellent match for her own wisdom and discretion.'

Disdaining his flattery, Clytaemnestra said, 'I wish to hear nothing more of this until I receive the distressing news of my bard's departure from this life. After that it will be time for you and I to speak together again. By then I will have decided whether the time is ripe for Aegisthus to return to Mycenae. Is that understood?'

'Perfectly.' Nauplius hesitated. 'But I was thinking . . .'

'There is some difficulty?'

'Aegisthus will be risking a great deal in this matter.'

'Nothing great is achieved without risk.'

'Quite so! But as things stand he will have only my word for this.'

'He knows you for his friend, does he not?'

'Yet he may ask for more. Is there not perhaps some token you might send to him as an earnest of your interest in his future welfare?'

She saw at once what the man was after. Should things go amiss, any identifiable token given as a pledge would render her complicit in the death of Pelagon, and it had always been her policy to keep such things deniable. Yet in an intrigue as perilous as this the demand was not unreasonable.

Clytaemnestra slipped from her finger a ring on which two jewelled serpents were entwined. 'This once belonged to a Lydian queen. My husband sent it to me some time ago with a letter informing me of his great victory at Clazomenae. Give it to Aegisthus. Tell him that it belonged to one of his forebears, as once did Mycenae itself. It is all the earnest he needs.' Dropping the ring into Nauplius' outstretched palm, she said, 'Conceal it about your person and leave this city at once. And do so in a way that makes it plain to all that you have incurred my displeasure.'

Smiling, Nauplius bowed his head.

'Play your part well,' she said, 'and I shall play mine. In good time both of us will have our satisfaction.'

But when he looked up again, Clytaemnestra had already turned her attention back to the wax tablet. It might suit her purposes for her husband to die in Phrygia but there was no relying on it, and it was no part of her plans that he should be defeated at Troy and return empty handed. She was thinking, therefore, that if his army was not to be trapped between Priam's host and the Hittite Empire, Agamemnon must be swiftly informed of the changing situation. So even before Nauplius had bowed out from her chamber, she was ringing the small silver bell that would summon her scribe.

The Last of Troy

Menelaus was woken from a fitful sleep by the trembling of the earth beneath his bed. For a few seconds, expecting the painted walls to collapse around him, he lay listening to the deep grinding roar, feeling it shake his lips and skin. Then there was only dust falling through the silence.

After a time he heard shouting outside and the noise of his own Spartan soldiery as they scrambled to get out of the building. He knew that the tremor might have been no more than a shrugging of the ground before the earth opened up beneath him. He knew that he too should make haste to get out into the clear. But he could not bring himself to move. Listening to the noise of the quake had been like listening to the stupefying pain of the world, and it was too much for him. He lay motionless on the bed feeling as if the moral lethargy that had seized his heart since entering this city had now infected every limb.

Yet the question that had kept him awake for most of the night remained unanswered: having already failed to kill his wife in the heat of passion when he discovered her in bed with Deiphobus at her side, how could he bring himself to kill her in cold blood?

Yet it would have to be done. Once he stood before the host with all that mighty pressure of expectation fixed on him, he would have no choice but to bring the sword down – just as

Agamemnon had been left with no choice when he stood before the host at Aulis. Thousands of men had already died in this war. They had died for the sake of his honour, and if the sack of Troy was the chief reward for those who had come through, the recapture of Helen was certainly another. And because no single one of them could be allowed to take her for himself, all must have the satisfaction of watching her die. Menelaus had assented to that judgement and it must be carried out. It must be done that day.

As he lay striving with these thoughts, he became aware of a sound somewhere outside the room in which he had slept alone. Someone was pummelling on a door with both fists and the knocking was going unanswered. Menelaus got up from the bed, pulled his cloak about his shoulders and went out into the hall. Everyone had rushed from the building for fear it might collapse – everyone but himself and Helen who was hammering at the locked door along the corridor. Her voice was muffled by its thickness but he could hear her crying to be let out.

Menelaus crossed to the door, unlocked and opened it. Helen saw his broad figure blocking the doorway, his face expressionless, his features darkened in the gloom by the greying, gingery beard which covered the familiar scar across his cheek. He was almost a stranger to her now.

When he said nothing she gasped, 'We have to get out of here. You must let me out. Please . . . I'm very afraid.'

'Does it matter so much,' he said dully, 'whether you die now or later?'

Her lips were quivering. She lifted a hand to her mouth. He heard the whimper of her breath behind it. 'Help me, Menelaus,' she whispered. 'You know me. You've always known the depths of my fear.'

'You were not afraid to betray me.' His voice was measured and cold. 'You were not afraid to flee from Sparta and bring shame on my house.'

'But that's not true,' she came back quickly. 'I was terrified. Every step of the way I was in mortal dread.'

'Yet you didn't let fear stop you.'

'I lacked the power. I was in the hands of a god.'

'You are in the hands of a god now. If Poseidon wants us he will certainly take us.' Scornfully he shook his head. 'In any case, any lying whore might claim as much.'

'I have wronged you,' she gasped, 'I freely acknowledge it. But not once, never once in my whole life, have I ever lied to you.'

He saw the truth of it in her eyes. Helen was shivering in her night-shift but her chin was held high. The silence of the plundered mansion waited round them. Sensing his uncertainty, she said, 'Did you think I was lying when I implored you not to leave me alone with him, when I begged you to let me accompany you to Crete that day?'

His hands had clenched into fists. He made to turn away from her, to shut the door on her again, but words crowded at his lips demanding to be spoken. 'In the name of all the gods, Helen, we were happy together in Sparta,' he heard himself saying. 'Our life was good. We ruled together over a contented kingdom. We had our child, the child we loved — the child that you abandoned.'

He might have struck her with the words.

Helen stared up at him, trembling. 'And can't you see that the guilt of it has tormented me all my days?' she cried. 'Do you think I will ever forgive myself?'

Confronting the full scale of her pain for the first time, he felt his own heart shaking. His eyes were casting about the darkness of the room, looking for his rage. He found only confusion.

'Yet you threw it all away,' he gasped. 'And for what? For what?'

At a loss to offer any explanation of a choice she had long since come to regret, Helen shook her head. 'It was madness,' she whispered. 'When Paris came to Sparta he was already possessed by the madness of Aphrodite. Her madness was too strong for me.'

'And Deiphobus?' he demanded. 'Do you blame the goddess for that too?'

'I blame her for nothing. We are what we are and must answer for ourselves.' Hope was absent from her voice, yet when her eyes looked up at him again they were filled with entreaty. 'But there are powers stronger than reason, Menelaus. Are you sure that such a power doesn't have you in its grip right now?'

His hands opened, and closed again, grasping at the air.

'Enough,' he said. 'What kind of fool do you take me for?'

'I have never thought you a fool,' she said. 'I have never believed you to be anything other than the truest and kindest of men. All the folly in this was mine.'

He stood uncertainly, confronted by both her pathos and her honesty. She had not yet asked for his forgiveness but if, as he suspected was about to happen, Helen fell to her knees and did so, he could no longer be sure that his heart would not vacillate. Quickly he sought to harden it.

'I've heard enough of this. Come noon today you'll have the justice of the gods. And so will I. So will I.'

He was about to close the door on her then, locking her in with her guilt and fear, with all her tragic beauty; but through a sudden catch in her breathing emerged a single, urgently uttered word: 'Wait.'

Menelaus stopped, knowing that he should not stop. Unable to prevent himself from hoping that a thing might still be said that would bring their whole wretched story to a better end, he turned to look back at the wife he had loved as he had never loved anyone else before or since.

Helen stood before him with her hands clasped together at her mouth and her shoulders hunched as though hugging herself against the cold.

'No one can escape the justice of the gods,' she whispered. 'What I hope to find is their mercy.'

In the dream Odysseus had come home to Ithaca and Penelope was running towards him down the cliff-path to the bay where his ship was moored. He had jumped over the side into the waves and was walking ashore through the surf to greet his wife with open arms, but as she approached more closely her face fell. She halted in her tracks. He saw her eyes gaping with horror. Puzzled, he looked down, following the direction of her gaze, and saw that the hands and arms he held out to hold her were still drenched with blood. He watched it dripping from his fingers. He saw it staining the water round his thighs. Looking back at his wife, opening his mouth to explain, he saw at once that words could make no difference – such an embrace of blood could never be acceptable. Penelope stood transfixed, shaking her head, holding up her white palms in a gesture of self-protection. Then the sea was rising and his balance was gone. With shocking force, salt-water slapped and splashed around him. Odysseus jumped awake aboard his lurching ship.

Unable to bear the smell of death in the city, he had decided to sleep on his ship where it lay moored on a strand of the bay. But a freak wave thrown up by the tide must have lifted the vessel where it stood on its keel and tipped him from his pallet to the scuppers amidst a boil of surf. Still emerging from the vague region between dream and waking, Odysseus heard how the dark sea sizzled and hissed across the turbulent bay. Then he took in the grinding of the earth beneath the rattle of shingle and knew that Poseidon had stirred.

When the strand was still again, he stumbled to his feet, looking towards the city. In the sulphurous light of the dawn sky it was impossible to tell from that distance how much more damage Troy had suffered. And then, so vivid had been the impact of his dream, he glanced down at his arms, expecting to find them still running with blood. He stood for a time, shaking his head, puzzling over the strange elision between the dream and the world. Had he been dreaming of water before the wave broke over him? Had his dream in fact invoked the wave, or had the sea pre-empted his dreaming mind?

Because there was no answer to such questions they left him uneasy, and he felt queasier still at the thought that the dream was Poseidon's work.

Once, long ago in Sparta, he had called down the curse of Earth-shaker Poseidon on all who failed to defend Menelaus's right to take Helen as his bride. But the oath had been sworn on the joints of a horse that had come reluctantly to the sacrifice, and from the moment in which he was required to swear it himself, Odysseus had suspected that the oath must come home to haunt him.

And so it had proved. Once again, as had been the case countless times since leaving Ithaca, Odysseus was tormented by the memory of the conversation in which his wife Penelope had perceived with devastating clarity the bind in which he found himself.

'So I am to understand,' she had said, 'that you devised this oath as a means to help my uncle Tyndareus solve the problem of choosing a husband for Helen without antagonizing all the other contenders for her hand?'

'That was my intention, yes.'

'And you did so on the understanding that Tyndareus would then persuade my father to countenance accepting you as my husband?'

'I did it for you.' he urged. 'You know how bitterly your father was opposed to me. I thought his brother's counsel might change his mind. And the plan worked.'

'Except that you too swore the oath,' Penelope reminded him.

'Palamedes insisted on it before all the others. I could hardly refuse. And there seemed to be no risk. No one was about to provoke the anger of the god by breaking the oath. As far as I could see, there was no reason why Menelaus and Helen should not be left to live happily in peace.'

'But you don't always see as far as you think you can see. And now the oath you devised to bring us together is tearing us apart.'

It was true, and the truth was underwritten by the logic of the gods who have an insatiable taste for irony. So for ten years Odysseus had devoted all his resources to winning this war, yet his heart had never truly been in it. Not when his twelve ships set sail from Ithaca, leaving Penelope alone on the cliff with the infant Telemachus in her arms. Not when he was luring the young Achilles to abandon his wife and child on Skyros in order to win undying glory in the war. Not when he finally contrived the death of Palamedes, whom he had always hated in his secret heart far more than he hated any of the Trojans. Nor even when he conceived the stratagem of the Wooden Horse as a means for the host to find its way inside walls so strongly built that they might stand for ever. And least of all now when he saw how all his efforts to negotiate a sane surrender of the city had been betrayed.

Odysseus had come to the war with only one intention – to return home as quickly and as profitably as possible to his wife and son. But as he stood in the thin light beside his toppled ship, with the waters of the bay shaking around him, he was possessed by a sickening conviction that returning home might prove as arduous as winning the war had been. And the man who returned to Ithaca would not be the man who had left; and who could blame his wife if she could not find it in her heart to welcome the grim stranger he had now become?

Agamemnon came down from what had once been King Priam's bedchamber to find his men jumpy and anxious to be gone. Having been woken from a drunken sleep by the shaking of the earth, they were afraid that the ground might move beneath them again with greater force. A bitter wind was blowing across the city. Through the livid dawn light, clouds heavy with rain hurtled low above Mount Ida. Some of the Argive ships which had been loosely beached on the night of the invasion bobbed and yawed in the turbid waters of the bay. Others had been knocked from their stays by the wave that came with the quake. Mariners were already down there, assessing the damage to masts and spars, or putting out in fishing smacks to retrieve the vessels that had broken loose. Everywhere he looked Agamemnon sensed the growing agitation to be gone from Troy.

He felt it himself. This city belonged to the dead now not to him. Impervious to everything, having endured the last indignity of a callous death, they had scarcely stirred in their piles while the ground trembled under them. And there were too many to move. Even if anyone had the stomach for the task, it would take days to clear the streets and burn all these corpses and there was still looting to be done.

Meanwhile the shrieks and moans of the women captives had begun to play on Agamemnon's nerves. He was standing at the wall of the citadel looking down across the lower city when Calchas came striding towards him, staff in hand, with Antenor at his side, grim-faced and recalcitrant. They were the last people he wanted to deal with now, but they had taken advantage of the confusion caused by the earth-tremor to force an encounter and there was no escaping them.

'Is this how the High King of Argos keeps his word?' Antenor demanded. 'Are we to believe that boys and pitiful old men went down fighting rather than plead for their lives? There are ten thousand ghosts in Troy. I pray that every one of them will come out nightly from the Land of Shades to haunt your dreams.'

'If your friends are dead,' Agamemnon growled, 'it's because you gave them into my hands.'

'On the strength of your word that their lives would be spared.'

'War is war, Antenor. You are king in Troy now. Learn what it means to be a king. If you would rule men, make them fear you first.'

'There's no one left for me to rule,' Antenor almost shouted the words back at him. 'Troy is dead. It's become a city of the dead. I have no desire to be a king of corpses.'

'Then go your ways, man, and count yourself lucky that you have your life still.'

Confronted by such indifference, Antenor's will collapsed in that moment. Helplessly he opened his hands and all the agony of Troy was resumed in his voice as he gasped, 'I can't find my wife. I've looked for her everywhere.'

Again Agamemnon snorted. 'I've had trouble enough these past ten years pursuing my brother's wife. I have no time to look for yours.'

Calchas said, 'Theano is priestess to Athena. Her person is sacred to the goddess.'

'Then let the Goddess protect her. She's no business of mine.' Agamemnon turned to stride away but he had taken only a few paces when he was halted by the cold authority in the priest's voice.

'The High King would do well to take care how he speaks of the gods. Already they begin to turn away from him.'

A tangle of broken veins flushed at Agamemnon's cheeks. He turned to glower at Calchas with narrowed eyes. 'Are you threatening me with curses, priest?'

'Earth-shaker Poseidon has already made his displeasure plain,' Calchas answered. 'The omens now say that he has made his peace with Athena.'

'Divine Athena has always taken my side.'

'There has been sacrilege in her temple,' Calchas answered. 'Her image has been plundered. Her priestess is missing. And the gods pursue their own ends,' he added quietly, 'not ours.'

Agamemnon's rage combusted then. 'The gods have given this great city into my hand. What clearer message do you need of their favour?'

'What the gods give,' Calchas answered, 'they can also take away.'

'The same holds true of kings,' Agamemnon snarled. 'If you value my favour, Calchas, you'd better look for more propitious omens. And you, Antenor – be certain of this – Troy, as you truly say, is dead. Before we Argives leave this land we shall do what Heracles and Telamon failed to do. We shall tear down these walls, stone by stone, so that they can never rise to trouble us again. Priam is no more. His seed is extinguished from the earth. We have seen the last of Troy. Now there is only one King of Men.' Agamemnon stood panting in his rage. 'Be thankful for his mercy.'

Then he turned away again, shouting for Talthybius. 'Call my captains together,' he demanded of the herald. 'I want them all in council. The last of the looting must be done by noon and the ships loaded. Then the host will gather at the Scaean Gate to witness Helen's execution. As soon as she's dead and the offerings are made, every ship's company will start work demolishing these walls; and once they're razed to the ground, the city will be put to the torch. I want to see nothing here but smoking ash and rubble. Then, and only then, shall we make sail for Argos.'

An hour later all the captains except Odysseus and Menelaus were gathered in the ransacked throne room of Priam's palace where they were waiting for Agamemnon to appear. Though the earth had not shifted again, Acamas and Demophon hovered uneasily within reach of the doorway. Even garrulous old Nestor was unusually silent except when he muttered impatiently about this waste of time. He demanded an explanation of the delay from Talthybius, but the herald merely glanced away, answering that the High King was in conference and would join them shortly.

'In conference with who?' Acamas asked dryly.

But before Talthybius could speak, Demophon said, 'Or is he still making his offerings on Cassandra's altar?'

Diomedes was sitting at the edge of the huge round hearth, nursing a thick head from the previous night. Impatient of the younger men's laughter, he demanded to know where Menelaus and Odysseus had got to, and whether there was to be a council that morning or not?

'Word has gone out among the Ithacans to bring Odysseus here,' the herald answered. 'He should join us quite soon. As for the King of Sparta . . .'

'The King of Sparta is here.'

All the men in the room turned to look at Menelaus who stood between the twin pillars of the doorway, wrapped in a vermilion cloak, his face anxious and drawn. 'Where is my brother?'

'The High King has not yet deigned to join us,' Diomedes scowled.

Menelaus nodded, sensing the impatience in the room. 'It's just as well. I need to speak with him before this council meets.'

'I wouldn't interrupt him just yet if I were you,' Demophon smirked.

But Menelaus was already making his way through the hall and up the stairs to the upper floor. He came out onto the wide landing just as Agamemnon emerged from the apartment where he had been alone with Cassandra since returning from his encounter with Antenor and Calchas.

'All right, I'm coming,' the King muttered gracelessly, brushing back his hair with big hands. 'Is everybody here?'

'I need to talk to you –' Menelaus said, '– privately, before you go down.'

Agamemnon appraised his brother with narrowed eyes, sensing his urgency. 'Is something wrong?' Without answering, Menelaus followed him into the apartment where he saw the slight, dark figure of Cassandra pulling on a dressing-gown as she walked past the open inner doorway of the bedchamber. He looked at his brother, who nodded and crossed the room to shut the inner door.

'Well, what is it?' Agamemnon frowned.

Swallowing, Menelaus said. 'I have changed my mind.'

'What do you mean – you've changed your mind?'

'About Helen.'

Agamemnon's face darkened. 'It's too late to hand her over to the Spartans, if that's what you're thinking. The word has already gone out that Helen will be executed here at Troy. It's what you led me to understand would happen and the entire host is now expecting it. I'm not about to disappoint them.'

Menelaus said, 'You don't yet understand me. There will be no execution. Not here and not in Sparta. Helen will not die. Not by my hand or by anybody else's. We are reconciled, she and I.'

Agamemnon stared at his brother in disbelief. Visibly his breathing quickened. He looked around the room as if to make sure that he was quite awake and all of this was actually happening.

His nostrils flared, but still, as he walked towards a table where his unbuckled sword-belt lay, he said nothing. He stood for a time, patting the table with the flat of his hand. Then he looked back at his brother with a thin, derisive smile at his lips.

'You are reconciled?'

'Yes.'

'I see,' Agamemnon nodded. 'So you asked your brother to raise all the armed might of Argos and bring it across the sea in a thousand ships so that we could spend ten miserable years fighting for your honour over a faithless wife who has humiliated and disgraced you, only to tell me that you've changed your mind?'

'This war was never about Helen,' Menelaus said quietly. 'No one knows that better than you. You wanted Troy's wealth and Helen gave you all the excuse you needed to seize it.'

Agamemnon glared across at his younger brother with violence in his eyes.

'Do you think I care nothing for the honour of the House of Atreus?' His voice was shaking as he spoke. 'Do you think I care nothing for you? Do you think I didn't wake in my sweat night after night thinking of how that cockscomb Paris was making a mockery of your name in every squalid tavern from Epirus to Ethiopia? Believe me, if Troy had been of no more account than a brigand's filthy rat-hole, I'd have crushed it just to show the world that no one lays a finger on anything that belongs to me or mine and gets away with it.' Agamemnon was panting now. 'And what return do I get for my loyalty? Apparently untroubled by the fact that your wife opened her legs for Paris, and then again for his brother Deiphobus and, for all I know, might have played the two-backed beast with old King Priam himself – untroubled by any of this, you stand before me like a sickly boy and tell me that you mean to take her back!' A vein throbbed at his temple as he shouted 'Have you gone quite mad? Have you lost all sense of honour?'

Menelaus stood with closed eyes under the withering assault.

His hands were clenched, his knuckles white as he said, 'There are things that count for more than honour in this world.'

Agamemnon brought his fist down on the table-top and shouted, 'Without honour a man is nothing. Nothing! He is less even than a worm. Men piss on those who do not prize their honour. In the name of all the gods, Menelaus, don't you remember what our father did to our mother when she betrayed him? Didn't you stand beside me watching her drown? Everyone there could see that Atreus loved the woman and that she had broken his heart, but he knew what his duty was to the honour of our house. He knew she had to die and that the world must watch her die.'

There were nights when still, as a grown man, Menelaus woke sweating with the anguish of that memory. He could clearly see the way his mother's hair had splayed beneath the surface, and how her breath bubbled from her open mouth, and the outline of her body wobbled in the green depths as though merging into water as the act of drowning protracted itself. His eyes were closed now, gripped in darkness, rejecting the memory as he had sought to do many times before.

Through clenched teeth he said, 'I am not our father.'

'Indeed you are not,' Agamemnon shook his head in disgust. 'Atreus would be ashamed to acknowledge you as his son.'

'If I am indeed his son,' Menelaus retorted. 'If either of us is, for that matter. Who knows who our father was? Certainly Atreus didn't, which is why he turned against us. Have you forgotten that? Or have you never dared to look it in the face?'

In fact, only silence filled the room, though it felt in that moment as though the whole space had burst into flame. Neither brother had ever admitted such a thought to the other since that night, nearly thirty years earlier, when the question of their paternity had first been raised. They were still small boys then, watching the quarrel between their father Atreus and his brother Thyestes, who had been vying for the throne of Mycenae after old king Sthenelus had died. When Atreus won the contest, Thyestes had vented his fury by poisoning all their minds.

'The throne might be yours now, brother,' Thyestes had shouted, 'but are you so sure about your sons? It may interest you to know that your Cretan whore of a wife has warmed my bed more times than I can remember while your back was turned.'

The boys had seen those drunken words cause the immediate banishment of Thyestes, the death by drowning of their mother Aerope, and the start of a gruesome cycle of vengeance that would contaminate their imaginations for the rest of their lives. Yet neither of them had spoken of them until now.

Trembling at what had happened, Menelaus snorted and glanced away. 'In any case,' he gasped, 'I would die sooner than become the monstrous sort of man that Atreus became.'

In a blaze of rage, Agamemnon seized the scabbard of his sword-belt in his left hand and drew the sword with his right. The blade hissed against the leather. His voice was shaking as he said, 'Humiliate yourself before me if you must, but I'll cut the breath out of your throat sooner than let you shame the House of Atreus before the host.'

Then the door to the bedchamber opened and Cassandra was standing in her robe, studying them, dark-eyed.

Without turning to look at her, Agamemnon crossed the room, holding the blade out before him till its point was pressing at his brother's throat.

'Tell me that you've heard me,' he said with a trembling fervour. 'Tell me that we'll shortly go down together and you will inform my captains that Helen's execution will take place before the Scaean Gate at noon.'

With the bronze point pressing so closely that it puckered the skin of his neck, Menelaus shook his head.

'Do this thing for me, brother,' Agamemnon gasped, his hand quivering a little, 'because I swear I will kill you if you do not.'

Menelaus said quietly, 'As our father was killed by the will of *his* brother?' He endured the menace in Agamemnon's gaze. 'Is that what you want – for the curse on our house to carry on looking for death after death down all the generations? Then kill me if you must. I can't prevent you and I have honour enough not to beg for my life.' He stood, panting with defiance. 'But this much I tell you: for all her frailties, I have always loved my wife. Even when I stood above her with a sword in my hand, I knew that I loved her and the knowledge was strong enough to stay my hand. Helen is as life itself to me. I've been a dead man all these long years since she left me. And I would rather die now than live without her for another day.'

Agamemnon stared along the blade of the sword in disbelief. A single panting sigh disturbed the spittle at his lips. Unable to countenance the unflinching gaze confronting him, he turned his head and looked, as if for guidance, to Cassandra, who observed the scene with an aloof, sibylline smile.

'What shall I do?' Agamemnon gasped.

Cassandra shrugged. 'Of all the Argives who came to Troy, this was the only man we had wronged. But you are the King. You must give him the justice you think fit.'

Absolving herself of the matter, she turned away into the inner chamber. The sons of Atreus were left alone together with the ghosts of their tormented ancestry beating about their heads. Downstairs the captains waited. The bitter wind blew across Troy, gusting in the alleys, disturbing the hair of the dead. And all that Agamemnon need do to make this wasteland complete was push the point of his sword into his brother's throat. The honour of the house would be served and men would fear his power all the more for having seen him take his brother's life. Meanwhile – he saw it almost as clearly as if the thought had summoned it – in some dark corner of the Land of Shades, the vindictive ghost of Thyestes would be smiling at this further harvest of the curse that had haunted their house since it had been founded, more than half a century ago, by the ruthless treachery of King Pelops.

The rage racing through Agamemnon's veins had become indistinguishable from pain. He was remembering how, as boys, he and Menelaus had sworn never to violate each other's trust. It was on the night when they had hidden in the darkness of the water stair at Mycenae before being smuggled out of the postern gate to seek refuge with Tyndareus in Sparta. Earlier that night their father Atreus had been murdered, Thyestes had seized his throne, and the two frightened boys could only vow always to be true to each other as they fled. But now, all these grim years later, after all they had endured, they had arrived at this bleak moment where Agamemnon stared at his brother in silence, trying to love him as a brother should love his brother and found that he could not.

But neither could he bring himself to murder him.

Agamemnon lowered the blade and threw it clattering across the room. 'Get from my sight,' he snarled. 'Take ship with your Spartan harlot if you must. But let neither of you ever set foot in Argos while I live.'

Having walked hurriedly in silence through the gathering of fractious and puzzled captains in the throne room, Menelaus came out of the palace just as Odysseus began to climb the steps towards him. Both men were dazed and distracted, staring at each other, almost as though struggling for recognition, like friends unexpectedly re-met after a separation of many years.

With the sudden, liberating realization that he was throwing off a shadow that had oppressed his life for far too long, Menelaus spoke first. 'This is well met,' he said. 'I couldn't have left Troy without speaking to you.'

Odysseus listened in bewilderment as Menelaus tried to explain himself, but so strong was the memory of this same man looming over Helen with a bloody sword in his hand that he found it difficult to take in what was happening.

'So Helen still lives?' he said.

'We are leaving together on the tide.'

'And Agamemnon knows this?'

Menelaus nodded, almost impatiently. 'Odysseus, I don't know if we'll ever meet again,' he pressed. 'Helen and I can never return to Argos after this.'

Again it took a little time for the truth of things to penetrate.

Odysseus felt a drizzle of rain blow at his face as he said, 'Where will you go?'

'I'm not sure. Eastwards I suppose. Perhaps to Egypt.'

Reflecting wryly on the ironies that seemed to rule all things now, Odysseus said, 'Then may the gods go with you.'

He would have walked on by, but Menelaus lifted a hand to prevent him. 'I have done you a great wrong,' he said. 'I should never have brought you out of Ithaca to this war. It was envy, more than need, that made me do so. Envy of the love that I saw between you and your wife.' Biting his lip, he looked up into his friend's troubled frown. 'When you get back home to her, tell Penelope that I beg her forgiveness.' Swallowing, he offered his hand.

Odysseus studied it with neither reproach nor sympathy in his eyes. Around them, on the steps of the palace and out across the square lay the lax bodies of the dead. From beyond the temple of Athena the head of the wooden horse looked down on them with a few tattered garlands still blowing from its mane. Menelaus saw the raindrops shining among the hairs of his friend's beard. Then he was amazed to hear Odysseus uttering a bitter chuckle as he walked away.

Aeacus had done his job well sixty years earlier when he built the walls at Troy, for as well as withstanding the shock of more than one earthquake they had resisted the longest siege in the history of warfare; and though the Trojans had themselves weakened one section when they broke open the masonry of the Scaean Gate in their eagerness to admit the wooden horse, everywhere else those gleaming limestone ramparts still stood strong. So it took longer than Agamemnon had hoped to tear them down.

As he laboured among his men, Odysseus was thinking that if the High King had given the matter any thought, he would have let the men of Troy live long enough to do this demolition job. As it was, the weary Argive army, anxious only to get away with its loot as quickly as possible, must now set to with rams and crowbars, battering and prising at the stones. Odysseus knew it was more than mere chance that his Ithacans had been assigned the formidable task of pulling down the eastern bastion with its deep well from which the citadel had drawn its water supply. The high brick superstructure had been toppled easily enough but as they chipped and heaved at the dressed stonework amidst a cloud of dust, Sinon could be heard muttering that this was what came of questioning the morality of that vindictive brute Agamemnon. Once a man's blood was shed, you couldn't squeeze it back in, he said, and the same held true for a whole host of corpses. Odysseus would have done better to keep his mouth shut rather than trying to salve his conscience by publicly arraigning the High King's ruthlessness.

Meanwhile, on the far corner of the bastion, Odysseus and Eurylochus were supervising an attempt to bring the masonry down by undermining it; but the foundations had been laid so deep, and the blocks were so large and closely fitted, that after an hour of digging they had made no larger profit from their work than to turn up the cracked skull, mottled bones and rotten leather corselet of some unlucky foot-soldier who had died in that place in an earlier war.

At the sight of that vacant skull, Odysseus was overwhelmed again by a black sense of the futility of human endeavour. Who could now tell how much wit and love and courage might have flourished inside that cup of bone before its owner came to fight and die beneath the walls of Troy? And the Troy at which he had fought was older than Priam's Troy, probably older than Laomedon's too. So how many wars must have been fought hereabouts, over how many centuries? And must another Troy rise one day above the rubble of these walls only to be destroyed in turn as some new army raised its might against the city? Did nothing change? And would his own skull be dug up like this one day, unrecognized?

The Lion of Mycenae was already congratulating himself that

his name must live for ever, and already the bards were at work, turning history into myth, slaughter into song; but as he stared back at the cracked eye-sockets of the skull, Odysseus looked forward only to the redeeming obscurity of a time in which there would be no living memory of the terrible thing that had been done at Troy.

So when Eurylochus broke the haft of his spade against another course of limestone footings and threw the useless tool away, grimacing up at Odysseus, he saw to his astonishment that his leader was standing above him, stripped to his breech-clout in the heat, with tears brimming at his eyes, as though the skull he held in the palm of his hand had once belonged to a well-loved friend.

Not till the late afternoon of the following day were they ready to set fire to the ruins of the city. All the women who were to be taken into captivity had been led away, wailing, to the ships. Everything of value that the ravaged capital had to offer was stowed in the holds beneath the oar-benches, and what the ships could not carry lay abandoned like so much rubbish on the strand or was dumped overboard in the choppy waters of the bay. Dry timber, bales of wool and straw and other combustible materials were arranged along the wider streets to encourage the spreading of the blaze, while men with scarves at their faces stacked the sullen multitudes of the dead in piles and dowsed them in oil. A wind rising to gale-force from the east promised to make the flames thrive even though the dense, swiftly moving storm-clouds threatened further rain.

Teams of men with torches started fires in every quarter and by dusk the whole noble city of Troy was one vast funeral pyre. The night sky flushed to an incandescent orange-red. The bruised clouds charred to ruddy-black above it. Smoke extinguished half the known stars, while new constellations of sparks gusted on the wind. Meanwhile, even where they stood at a far distance from the blaze to gaze with awe at what they had accomplished, the heat and stink of burning came at men's faces like a pestilence.

Odysseus was standing on Thorn Hill with his dark-skinned herald Eurybates, looking towards the inferno with shielded eyes when he saw Agamemnon's chariot hurrying across the plain towards him. As the driver reined in the sleek team of blacks that had once belonged to Paris, Agamemnon shouted up to Odysseus that he wanted to have words. Uncertain whether the tone of his voice was anxious or elated, Odysseus made his way down to where Agamemnon's horses sweated and fretted, rolling their eyes towards the roar of the inferno.

'I've been looking for you everywhere!' Agamemnon shouted. 'There's something I need to tell you. Something you need to know.' Odysseus was able to make out the gleam of triumph in his eyes. 'We've done the right thing. In destroying Troy, I mean. I'm sure of it now.'

'I thought you always were.'

'Well, yes, I was, of course.' Agamemnon frowned at his obdurate comrade. The buckles on his harness seemed to blaze in the reflection of heat from the burning city. 'But I've just had a despatch out of Mycenae and it confirms I was right. The Hittites are on the march. They're coming westwards, heading for Troy. They'll be here in a matter of days.'

'The Hittites? I thought they were still at war in the east.'

'I'm told that Hattusilis has settled things on his eastern front and now he's decided to send the whole western half of his army to the aid of Troy. He doesn't yet know that Priam's finished.'

Odysseus stood in silence for a time, taking in this unexpected development, thinking quickly. 'When was the despatch sent?' he asked.

'I'm not sure. Why?'

'Because Hattusilis may not have known that Troy had fallen when the pigeon was released, but if his spies are any good he'll know by now. Presumably he's not about to risk losing control of the Hellespont to Mycenaean power.'

'Exactly.' Agamemnon fixed Odysseus with his smirk. 'And if

we'd stuck with your plan we'd have a big new war on our hands any time now. A war I'm not at all sure we could win. Do you understand?'

'Yes,' Odysseus answered dryly, 'I understand.' He looked back at where one of the oil magazines under the citadel had just combusted with a whooshing roar of yellow flame. 'And the fact that you didn't know this when you decided to kill everyone in Troy is a matter of no moral consequence whatsoever, I suppose?'

Agamemnon flushed with exasperation. He had won a great victory, perhaps the greatest victory in the history of warfare, yet his own brother had frustrated him, his captains were increasingly truculent around him, and this man, his most trusted counsellor and one of his oldest comrades, evidently held him in contempt. Where was the justice in all this? Why would no one honestly acknowledge him for what he had proved himself to be, the King of Men?

'The fact is, I was right, wasn't I?' he demanded. 'We were stretched to the limit coping with Priam's western alliance. There was no way we could take on the whole Hittite Empire. So we've done well out of this. We're going back with all the treasure of Troy stowed in our holds. There's no danger of reprisal from this pile of ash and rubble, and Hattusilis will be content to keep his Asian empire intact. He won't risk crossing the Aegean to avenge Priam any more than we're about to outstare him here. By the time his army reaches Troy our ships will be well gone. The Hittites are welcome to what's left after this fire has burned out!'

Odysseus stood in silence, letting the bluster blow past him. When it was done, he turned away and called up to his herald. 'Do you hear this, Eurybates? It seems that the High King has come to crow over me.' Then he glowered back at Agamemnon. 'Is that it?'

'No, that's not it,' Agamemnon scowled. 'I came here as an act of friendship. I came to tell you this because I thought it might ease that delicate conscience of yours. Think about it, man. Can you believe that Antenor and the Dardanians would have stayed loyal to your treaty once the Hittites turned up with a force large enough to drive us into the sea?' Before Odysseus could answer, he pointed upwards over the Ithacan's shoulder. 'Look! Do you see what that is?'

Odysseus turned his head and saw where a bonfire had burst into a bright conflagration against the blackness of the night sky on the summit of Mount Ida.

'It's the first of the chain of signal fires.' Agamemnon's eyes were themselves smouldering with pride. 'In a minute or two the detachment on Lemnos will see it and light their fire, and from there the signal will leap to the rock of Zeus on Mount Athos, and then it'll be passed on from beacon to beacon till all Argos knows that Troy has fallen.' Agamemnon looked back with a smile of satisfaction. 'The gods know that we've done what we came here to do.' But when he failed to find any sign of assent in the anguished intelligence of the face across from him, he shook his head impatiently. 'You're a dreamer, Odysseus! You're a dreamer and I'm glad of it. I doubt there's another man on earth who could have thought up the stratagem of the wooden horse. So everything we've loaded in our ships we owe to you and your imagination. I don't deny it for a moment, and I thank you for it. I thank you from the bottom of my heart. But admit it, man – if we'd tried to handle things the way you wanted, we would have ended up with nothing. We'd have been lucky to save our skins from the Hittite host. So remind yourself of what's stowed in your ships and be grateful for your good fortune. Then go back home to Penelope in the knowledge of a job well done. That's what I came to say. If you've any sense, you'll sleep well tonight because of it.'

Without waiting for a response, Agamemnon signalled to his driver to turn the chariot away. Odysseus watched it speed across the plain, a fleeting dark shadow against the fierce, incendiary glare in which, hour by hour, the city of Troy was vanishing from the face of the earth. Meanwhile, high at his back, the beacon on

Mount Ida proclaimed to the world in tongues of flame that the King of Men was victorious and nothing would ever be the same again.

The Ghosts of Mycenae

The drowned body of the bard Pelagon was found washed up on the shore of an uninhabited island in the bay of Argos. The last time he'd been seen alive he was in the company of a young Corinthian poet of conspicuous beauty who had come as a pilgrim to the court at Mycenae declaring himself to be a passionate admirer of Pelagon's art. At the young man's suggestion the two bards had taken a small boat out onto the gulf for a pleasure cruise. But some misadventure must have happened, a freak gust of wind driving them onto a shoal perhaps, for the wreckage of their craft was discovered later that day with no one aboard.

Because the Corinthian's body was never recovered, a degree of mystery and scandal surrounded the affair. But Queen Clytaemnestra ordered a time of mourning in Mycenae, not least because the chief bard's regrettable death left unfinished the great Lay of Agamemnon on which he had been working for many years. The High King's eventual return from Troy would be, she insisted, the poorer for the lack of it.

Not long afterwards a traveller turned up in Mycenae, bearing rich gifts and asking for an audience with the Queen. Aegisthus had been only a boy of twelve when he fled the city more than twenty years earlier, so no one recognized this suave, intense stranger as the son of Thyestes, who had ruled Mycenae for a number of years until Agamemnon and Menelaus, the vengeful sons of Atreus, had returned with the Spartan army at their backs to reclaim their father's throne. So if there was some surprise that the stranger was speedily granted the private audience he sought, there was no immediate understanding, even among the better-informed citizens, that the blood-drenched course of Mycenaean history was about to undergo a further violent change.

'That you were powerful I already knew,' said Aegisthus, settling himself on the proffered couch, 'and King Nauplius warned me at some length that you are also formidably intelligent. But he neglected to inform me that you have the further advantage of being a very beautiful woman.'

Knowing that she was some years older than the refined man across from her, and that he must already have enjoyed much success with younger women on whose faces the cares of state were not indelibly inscribed, Clytaemnestra raised a languorous hand to brush the remark aside. 'There is no appetite for flattery here,' she said. Yet it was evident in her smile that she was not displeased.

Exiled from power by his father's defeat and death, Aegisthus had clearly learned that the attractive exercise of charm might supply many deficiencies of a fugitive's life. His vivid blue eyes were still smiling as he said, 'Nor was there any thought of flattery here. On the contrary, I understand very well that my only hope of leaving Mycenae alive resides in your respect for my honesty as one who has also suffered at your husband's hands.'

'So you believe you have my measure already? And what if you are wrong?'

'Then at least I will have died proudly trying to recover what is mine.'

'Rather than running from bolt-hole to bolt-hole ahead of Agamemnon's men?' Clytaemnestra gave a little, humourless laugh. 'My husband left me with very clear instructions. *Aegisthus is as dangerous as his father was,* he warned me. *Hunt him down while I'm gone and, once you have him in your power, show him no mercy.'* And then, almost as though this were a matter on which she should take his advice, she asked, 'Was he right, I wonder? Is that what I should have done?'

Opening his hands, Aegisthus said, 'Doubtless that would have been the proper course, if you were no more than an obedient wife. But I imagine you have always prided yourself on being rather more than that.'

'Yet you should understand,' Clytaemnestra arranged the many folds of her viridian gown, 'that once my agents traced you to the court of that sickly weasel on Euboea, you would not have lasted long if I didn't have a use for you.'

Unfazed, Aegisthus studied her with admiring eyes. 'I always considered Agamemnon a fool. Now I know he was never more so than when he failed to secure your loyalty.'

There was no arrogance, merely a casual acceptance of simple fact, in the Queen's nod of assent. 'Yet there was a time when he could count on my absolute support,' she said, 'in matters of state at least.'

'But Aulis changed all that?'

Clytaemnestra sighed. 'It began long before then, but yes, at Aulis everything changed.'

'Not only the wind,' he dared.

'No, not only the wind.'

'And you are no longer obedient?'

'Oh yes,' she said, 'but not to Agamemnon.'

'Then to whom?'

'Not to any man, I assure you.'

'A god then?' He paused for a moment over the severity of her frown. 'Or a goddess perhaps?'

Though she said nothing, he caught a glint of acknowledgement in her eyes.

'I confess that my own devotions are to Divine Artemis,' he volunteered. 'I intend to make offerings to her while I am here, in the hope that she will look with more favour on Mycenae.'

For a moment Clytaemnestra had felt transparent under the glitter of those eyes, as if he had looked into the cold cave of her heart and seen the altar at which she worshipped there. Only then did she understand just how dangerous this man might be. Beneath his charm lurked a soul that had been forged in a dark smithy. It further occurred to her that the two of them together resembled the twisted serpents on the ring she had given him for a pledge, the ring which Aegisthus was fingering conspicuously now as he smiled across at her. It was time she took control of this conversation.

'You must not imagine,' she said coolly, 'that I am unaware of your following here in Mycenae. I know that not everyone in this city rejoiced when my husband overthrew your father. There are those here who still think of you as their rightful prince.' She paused before adding, almost as an afterthought, 'Their names are known to me.'

Because some instinct of his survivor's soul had already detected a kindred air of corruption in this woman, Aegisthus smiled. It was to that corruption he spoke when he answered with a lightness that surprised her, 'But not to your husband?'

'Not yet. Their lives are in my hands, not his. As is, of course, your own.'

The smile dissolved at his lips. He waited for a moment, gazing at her with an intensity that she would have found impertinent in any other man. 'Then I think,' he declared quietly, 'that it has found its destined home.'

Both voice and eyes were so patently sincere that she was astonished by the utterance. Either this man was a consummate actor or, and with every moment this began to feel more likely, he had been brought here not merely at her behest but by his own unshakable sense of destiny. Not a word she had spoken had surprised him. Still less had it made him afraid. By some divinatory power born of a lifetime spent on the perilous edge of things he seemed to know her soul almost as intimately as she did herself.

Already they were deeply complicit, twinned serpents capable of renewing each other's life, or of ending it with a toxic kiss.

Her own instinct had been true then. Here was exactly the accomplice she needed for the most dangerous enterprise of her career. And if, for a moment, she had almost been in awe of this man, Clytaemnestra now felt an equivalent power rising inside her like a snake.

From a silver mixing bowl chased with a design of nymphs and satyrs, she poured wine into two goblets and crossed the room to sit closer to Aegisthus. 'Now you will tell me about yourself,' she smiled. 'I want to hear your whole story. In particular I wish to know what feelings passed through you as a child on the night when you murdered King Atreus.'

'But I cannot tell my story,' he returned her smile, 'without also telling my father's; and that cannot be done without raising all the ghosts of Mycenae.'

'Then raise them,' she said. 'Let me hear what they have to say.'

So nightmarish was the story Aegisthus had to tell that, when she thought about it afterwards, Clytaemnestra was uncertain whether his cool, ironical voice made it harder or easier to accept its appalling truth; for in the dangerous smile on his handsome face could be seen the latest flowering of a curse that had haunted his family since his grandfather's time. So much power had accrued to old King Pelops that most of the mainland of Argos was eventually named for him, but that power was won by treacherous means, and the curses he invoked were passed on, like evil seed, from one generation to the next. So Aegisthus told how even before the death of Pelops, his estranged sons, Atreus and Thyestes, who had fled the shadow of their imperious father to seek fortunes of their own, were set against one another by that legacy of curses. Their quarrels came to a head when Atreus was made king of Mycenae. Furious at being cheated of his own claim to the Lion Throne, Thyestes exposed his brother's wife Aerope as his whore, thus calling the paternity of Agamemnon and Menelaus into question; and though Atreus eventually recalled his brother from the banishment to which he consigned him, it was only with the intention of perpetrating the most horrific act of vengeance that his mind could conceive.

Thyestes, of course, was unaware of this. Delighted by his brother's change of heart, he returned to his wife and children in Mycenae. That night he was treated as the guest of honour in the banqueting hall of the Lion House and made a good meal of the delicious stew that was served up for him. Assuring him that he had not yet tasted the daintiest portions, Atreus pressed him to eat more. Another salver was placed before him and, when the lid was lifted, Thyestes found himself staring in bewilderment at a neatly arranged pile of little hands and feet. They lay in the blood that had leaked from them, small bones and severed gristle protruding from raw, vividly red flesh. Then his eyes were caught by the splashes of silver paint on the tiny fingernails that his four-year-old daughter had held up for his admiration on his arrival home in Mycenae only a few hours earlier.

'Can you imagine how Atreus smiled as the colour drained from Thyestes' face?' Aegisthus said. 'Think how cold his voice must have been when he said, "Console yourself with this thought, dear brother – the confidence that my sons are indeed my own has been stolen from me; but from this hour forth, you will never be in any doubt that you and your children will always be one flesh." But by then, I suppose, Thyestes must already have been out of his mind with the shock of what had been done to him. And what loathing for his own body must such knowledge have stirred? Yet he was condemned to live with it as he fled from Mycenae. Nor did Atreus himself emerge from that hideous banquet with his mind unscathed. Increasingly he grew obsessed by guilt at the thing he had done. His dreams became so troubled that he scarcely dared sleep at night. Then his anxieties increased when a long drought parched the countryside for miles around the city. Weeks passed without rain; the crops withered in the fields. When the harvest failed and famine threatened everyone's survival, Atreus succumbed to the general belief that his dreadful crime was the cause of the disaster. Under pressure from the city's priesthood, he was driven to consult the oracle at Delphi for guidance on how best to cleanse himself of the pollution of that crime. He was told it could be done only by recalling Thyestes to Mycenae.'

At that point Aegisthus left a silence in which he composed himself to speak of the circumstances surrounding his own birth, for in all his years of exile he had never previously confided in anyone. He might have found it impossible now had he not been urged on by this queen's insatiability for truth.

Sensing his uncertainty, Clytaemnestra said, 'My own life is well acquainted with horror. We are kindred in that, you and I. The truth can only bring us closer.'

Aegisthus smiled in assent and went on to tell how Thyestes had sought refuge at the court of King Thesprotus in Sicyon. On a visit to that city many years earlier he had fathered a daughter who had since grown up to become priestess to Divine Athena. Though he had not seen her since she was a babe in arms, it was to Pelopia that Thyestes now turned for consolation. Afraid that she must instinctively recoil from him as he recoiled from himself, he was overwhelmed with gratitude at the unexpected warmth with which Pelopia received him.

'She was a consecrated priestess as well as his daughter,' Aegisthus said. 'Perhaps she came to believe that she could heal her father's troubled soul? Whatever the case, Thyestes began to nurse an unholy passion for this beautiful young woman who had brought hope to his blighted life. That passion became an obsession, and when Pelopia realized that her sympathy had been mistaken for some stronger emotion, she sought, as best she could, to withdraw.'

Sensing the agitation that must lie in the fissures beneath his dry, ironical regard, Clytaemnestra listened in fascination as Aegisthus went on to tell how Thyestes, denied his daughter's company, had taken to stalking her. On a night when she was due to make her offerings to Athena, he concealed himself in the shadows of a grove from where he could spy on the sacrificial rites. He watched in a state of intense excitement as she drew the knife across the throat of a black ewe. When the offering was made, Pelopia clapped her hands and led the temple maidens in the dance to the goddess. Thyestes saw her lose her footing as she slipped in a pool of blood that had drained from the severed arteries of the ewe. When she rose to her feet her tunic was splashed with stains. Covertly he followed her to watch her wash away the bloodstains in the temple fish-pond; and there, crazed by the sight of her nakedness, Thyestes masked his face with his cloak, pressed his sword at her throat to silence her, and took her by force.

He must have woken from that demented trance of passion to see his daughter sobbing on the ground beneath him. Dropping his sword, Thyestes backed away. Unable to speak, scarcely able to breathe, he turned and ran. With his mind descending into ever deeper turmoil, he kept on running until he was gone from Sicyon, and when he came to the sea he took ship for distant Lydia.

'Some days after Pelopia had been found in a dumb state of shock,' Aegisthus said, 'Atreus arrived in Sicyon looking for Thyestes. No longer virgin by then, and therefore no longer priestess to Athena, Pelopia had been taken into the king's care. When Atreus saw her sitting sadly in the court, he too seems to have fallen under the spell of her strangely familiar presence. Assuming that the girl was the king's daughter, he asked Thesprotus if he might take her for his new wife.

'For some time Thesprotus had been worrying over how to keep at bay the imperial might of his powerful neighbour in Mycenae, so he immediately saw the value of such an alliance. But he also knew that Atreus would recoil from the proposal if he learned the truth of what had happened to his ward. So Thesprotus cannily decided to say nothing of Pelopia's tragic fate. Atreus returned to Mycenae with his bride and nine months later Pelopia gave birth to a son.'

Aegisthus paused again, reaching for his wine. When he resumed, his voice was held under still colder control. 'Having already turned his back on Agamemnon and Menelaus,' he said, 'Atreus was delighted by the birth of a new heir. But shortly after recovering from her confinement, Pelopia took the baby from its crib and carried it into the hills around Mycenae where she left it to die. Imagine the consternation here in the Lion House! Atreus told himself that his young wife must have been over-whelmed by the madness that can sometimes possess a new mother. But as he sent out people to search for the child, he was fearful that the gods were still conspiring against him. To his enormous relief, the infant was found unharmed in the care of a goatherd who had given it to one of his nanny-goats for suckling.'

Clytaemnestra said, 'So that is how you came by your name!'

Aegisthus smiled. 'Atreus named me for the strength of the goat that had shown me more tender mercy than my mother did. And so, entirely unaware that my conception, birth and survival were all the work of a malignant fate invoked by a chain of curses binding one generation to the next, I grew up in the citadel at Mycenae as the half-brother and unloved companion of Agamemnon and Menelaus, who had withdrawn into a conspiracy of mutual support after the execution of their mother. As you can imagine, they did not greatly care for me!'

Looking at the man he had become, Clytaemnestra could see that even as a child Aegisthus must have been troublingly beauti-ful. His corn-coloured hair, intense, periwinkle eyes, and lean body, delicately boned but with the promise of an athlete's swift strength, would have contrasted with the brawnier, more rumpled features of his two stepbrothers. Accordingly they would have taken pleasure in informing him that he had the vacant eyes, rancid stink and doubtless the randy morals of the she-goat who had suckled him. Yet, however painful the insults he took, Aegisthus said, he remained confident that he was the favoured heir of Atreus. Sooner or later a day must come when he would be given the power to make his tormentors eat every word with which they had wounded him. In the meantime he was content to scheme alone, looking for ploys to darken their father's mind against them without ever appearing openly to do so.

Thyestes, meanwhile, had grown restless with his state of exile in Lydia. He was driven by the single obsessive thought that all the evil fortune in his life had been engendered by his brother Atreus. So Atreus must die. And when he was dead, Thyestes would seize the throne of Mycenae. And then there would be sanity and justice in the world again.

Seven years after he had fled from Sicyon to Lydia, Thyestes learned from traders putting in at Smyrna that discontent was rife in Mycenae. Long years of drought had taken a dreadful toll on the surrounding countryside. As crops failed and livestock perished, people murmured that no land had ever suffered such prolonged misfortune unless its king had offended the gods, and there could be no more monstrous crime than the one that Atreus had perpetrated on his brother. The pollution of that crime must be cleansed; but the oracle at Delphi had long ago proclaimed that the drought would not lift until Thyestes returned. So how much longer must the people wait for the god's demand to be answered?

Confident that the wind was now blowing in his favour, Thyestes took ship back across the Aegean. His intention was to put in at Euboea where King Nauplius, who had no love for Atreus, would give him shelter. From there he would proceed to Delphi and seek guidance on how best to avenge himself on his brother.

'At Delphi,' Aegisthus said, 'he received what was, perhaps, the strangest oracle ever pronounced by the god. *How else should a man take vengeance on his brother*, he was told, *except by raping his own daughter?*'

'But in his madness he had already done that,' Clytaemnestra said.

Aegisthus smiled. 'Which was exactly the confusing thought that came to my father when he heard the judgement of the god. Surely such madness could not be required of him again? So he came out of the temple into the glare of the day bewildered and dismayed, scarcely aware of his surroundings. And by a gesture of chance such as happens only through the will of the gods, he did so at just the moment when Agamemnon and Menelaus arrived in the forecourt of the temple. Atreus had sent them there to make placatory offerings on behalf of his stricken city. It was Menelaus who recognized Thyestes first. He pointed him out to Agamemnon who immediately commanded their guard to seize him. Thyestes was brought in fetters to Mycenae; but the gods were far from done with him.'

Aegisthus took a drink from the goblet which Clytaemnestra had replenished for him. 'As it happened,' he continued, Atreus was away from Mycenae at that time, putting down a band of brigands who were causing trouble on the Corinth road; so his sons threw Thyestes into the dungeon to await his return. I remember Agamemnon taunting me about their achievement, bragging that Atreus would now recognize who his true heirs were. They would soon be back in his favour, not some upstart goat-boy who belonged among the stinking shepherds who had found him . . . things of that sort. The oracle had been fulfilled. Thyestes had been brought back to Mycenae. The god had been obeyed. Soon the drought must be lifted. Surely Agamemnon must receive his father's thanks and praise! Imagine his disappointment, therefore, when Atreus merely nodded as though having difficulty digesting the fact that his brother was back in the city and that something must now be done about him. Though I was only seven years old, I saw at once that he could not bring himself to look in the face of the man he had so savagely wronged. Certainly, he could not bring himself to order his brother's death, even though he had no wish to see him live as a continual threat to his own security. And then I think that some god must have whispered in my ear that Atreus was in need of my help. In any case, I spoke up in the silence of the hall. "The oracle decreed that Thyestes must be brought back to Mycenae," I said. "It did not insist that he must be allowed to live. If my father wishes it, I will gladly put an end to his wretched life." I remember that

Atreus looked at me as though seeing me for the first time – a seven-year old boy confidently volunteering to commit murder as if it was the most natural thing on earth. But that was exactly how it felt to me.'

Conscious of the quickening of her heart, Clytaemnestra stared at her guest in fascination. Looking into those intense blue eyes, she had no difficulty imagining the peculiar innocence of the child who had uttered those terrifying words even though not a shred of that innocence was evident in the smile across from her.

'Of course, Agamemnon began to scoff immediately,' Aegisthus continued, 'but Atreus raised an imperious finger to silence him and asked if I would truly do this thing for him. "If the father I love desires it of me," I answered at once. And he said, "I do. I do desire it." And so the thing was decided. Agamemnon sought to protest, of course, claiming that such an important task would be safer in his own hands than those of a mere child. But he could only blush when Atreus demanded to know why he had not done the job already. Was it perhaps because Agamemnon believed that Thyestes was indeed his father?'

Aegisthus smiled at the irony of the gods. 'I think it must have been the first time that the question of Agamemnon's paternity had been so openly raised between them,' he added, 'for he blanched at the imputation and strode from the king's chamber in a blustering sulk of rage. I cannot now say which gave me the greater pleasure, to receive this earnest of the degree to which I was loved and trusted by Atreus, or to see my tormentor Agamemnon so roundly humiliated by the man he had sought to please. Either way, when Atreus offered me the loan of his own sword to do the deed, I proudly declared that my mother Pelopia had already given me a short sword as a portion of my birthright heritage from Sicyon. I was used to its weight, it could be concealed more easily in the folds of my cloak, and I would prefer to use it as the instrument of Thyestes' death. What I did not say was that the sword had exercised a powerful fascination over my mind ever since the solemn occasion when my mother first presented it to me. The bronze blade was finely chased with a hunting scene: a wild boar, a pack of hounds and men with spears; and the pommel was delicately fashioned in the form of the head of Artemis. I had never displayed the weapon in public where my half-brothers might learn to covet what was my most prized possession, and my heart was excited now by the thought of putting it to use in what must be the most noble of all causes, the defence of my father's life and honour.'

Aegisthus fell silent for a time. Aware that he was now approaching the climax of his story, Clytaemnestra poured more wine into his goblet. She watched him stare into its depths before drinking. She saw the shadows of memory move across his dark, angular features. She waited patiently for him to speak.

Without telling his mother what he was doing, the boy Aegisthus had taken his sword from its place of concealment and made his way down the stairway to the vaulted store-room beneath the citadel which served as a prison in those days. Having seen no one but his gaoler for days, Thyestes looked up at the unexpected sight of a small boy approaching him through the gloom with an oil-lamp in his left hand and his right hand tucked inside the folds of his cloak.

'We had never seen each other before,' Aegisthus said, 'and when he saw from my clothing that I was well-born he demanded to know whether another of his brother's brats had come to crow over him. I held the lamp so that I could study his face and was struck by his resemblance to Atreus. This man was younger, and there was a hungrier look about his cheeks and eye-sockets, but he was unmistakably the brother of the man who had sent me to murder him. He sat crouched against a wall that had been carved out of the solid rock, with his hands firmly tethered at the wrists and one leg shackled by a bronze chain fixed to a cleat in the wall. The store-room stank of his piss and shit. "You are my father's enemy," I said, "and I have come to put an end to your life." Of course Thyestes snorted at that, and shook his head as if to convince himself that he wasn't merely dreaming. But then I put the lamp down where it would shed most light and advanced towards him, taking my sword from the folds of my cloak. He said, "Is my brother so great a coward that he sends a child to do his dirty work these days?" Then he pulled himself up to his feet, saying, "Come on then, little boy, you'll be doing me a kindness." He held his bound wrists up above his head, exposing his stomach to my blade, but then, as I drew back the sword ready to plunge it deep into his flesh, he moved with surprising nimbleness, pushed his free leg between my own, and tripped me to the floor. The sword slipped from my grip and the next thing I knew this big, half-naked man was leaning over me with the hilt of the sword gripped in his bound hands staring down at me. "Shall I kill you then, spawn of Atreus," he said, "as Atreus killed my children and served their poor flesh up for me to eat?" I was staring up at him, wide-eyed, with the sword blade trembling above my throat. Then I heard him gasp as though he had been pushed from behind by a god. "Where did you get this?" he demanded. I lay beneath his weight, unable to grasp what was happening. He was staring not at me but at the head of Artemis on the pommel of my sword. "Where did you get this sword?" he shouted. "Tell me or I'll cut the tongue out of your head."

'Thinking he was accusing me of theft, I gasped out that the sword had been given to me by my mother. Immediately Thyestes demanded to know who my mother was. "Pelopia," I stammered, "daughter of King Thesprotus of Sicyon."

'He lowered over me more closely then, shaking his head as he scrutinised my face. "How old are you?" he demanded, and when I told him I was seven, I could see his mind working quickly behind his eyes. "And your mother is Pelopia?" He pressed the point of the sword to the skin of my neck. "You swear you are telling me the truth?" Terrified of this strange, violent man, I swore on my life that I spoke the truth and was amazed when he lifted his weight off me and stood trembling in the gloom. I would have scrambled away then but he held me down with his foot, demanding to know whether Pelopia knew that he was here in

Mycenae under confinement. I said that I didn't know for sure, but I didn't think so because she rarely left the women's quarters and Agamemnon had kept his prisoner secret as a surprise for Atreus when he returned. Then, "Listen to me, boy," Thyestes panted. "If you wish to live you must swear on the head of Divine Artemis here to do exactly as I say. Believe me, more than both of our lives may depend on it." Then he pushed the pommel of the sword into my hand and made me swear a terrible oath that I would obey him. As I stammered out the oath, I could hear the rasp of his breath. I could feel his skin trembling next to mine. "I know your mother," he said. "She is very dear to me. Bring her here to me now. Tell her that the father she once loved begs to have words with her."

'I lay in a state of confusion, wanting only to be out of that evil place, unable to understand what he could mean. But, "You have sworn," he growled. "You will bring a terrible fate down on your head if you fail to keep that oath. Now go. Go quickly. Bring Pelopia to me." He lifted his foot off my chest. I got up, unable to take my eyes off him. Then I turned and ran for the stairs.'

'And your mother,' Clytaemnestra said, 'tell me, how did she respond to this?'

Aegisthus faltered for a moment. 'My mother was a strange, fey creature, who rarely left her apartment unless it was to feed the birds or stare out across the hills as though in expectation of someone or something. And she was prey to fits of black depression, when she would speak to no one but me, even though I could understand almost nothing of what she said.' For the first time he looked up at the woman across from him with a pained frown. 'I loved her very much and was greedy for more of her love than she was able to give me; but I was also alarmed by her strange, distracted ways. And that night she was as confused as I was by what I had to tell her. For a time she would say nothing in answer to the questions I gabbled out. But when I told her of the dreadful oath I had been made to swear on the head of Artemis, she gathered her mantle about her shoulders and accompanied me, shivering all the way, down the dark stair to the dungeon.

'I watched as she peered through the lamp-lit gloom at the shackled man who stared back at her. Thyestes had used the edge of my sword to sever the tethers at his wrists and he was holding the sword still, so I was afraid for both of us. But though nothing was said for what felt like a very long time, it was immediately clear to me that they recognized each other. Eventually Thyestes croaked out my mother's name, almost as though he were asking her a question. I couldn't see my mother's face because it was buried at his shoulder but I caught the glisten of tears at his eyes. "Pelopia," he asked hoarsely, "this sword that you gave to your son, how did you come by it?"

'He was holding up the sword in the lamp-light so that she could see the pommel and the chased engraving on the blade. She turned her face away and then looked down at her feet as she said, "It was dropped by the stranger who raped me on the night when I last made the offering to Artemis at Sicyon." She reached out and took the sword from her father's hand. "The sword was his," she said, gazing down at the blade with revulsion in her eyes. "I gave it to my son in the hope that one day he might avenge my honour."'

Aegisthus drew in his breath. 'I knew nothing of any of this,' he said. 'I can only assume that my mother must have been waiting until I was nearer manhood before telling me her story. But the gods were impatient for the truth to be known. I was still trying to cope with the shock when I heard Thyestes say, "Pelopia, the sword is mine."'

Clytaemnestra saw Aegisthus wince at the memory. There came a long silence, which again, out of a tact that was now touched with a surprising measure of compassion for the tormented man across from her, she chose not to break.

'From that moment things are not so clear to me,' Aegisthus said eventually. 'I felt bewildered by the tension between them in that awful place. I was trembling and I could feel the hairs bristling at my neck as though I was in the presence of a god. Then even before I could understand what was happening, my mother had turned the sword on herself and with a single thrust pushed the blade deep into her stomach. I can see her body swaying as she stares up into Thyestes' face. He is looking back at her, reaching out his hands when she begins to fall. Then they are both slumped on the stone flags of the floor and I can see blood shining like oil in the lamp-light as it seeps into the cracks between the stones. I wanted to be gone from there to a place where I could tell myself that none of this had happened, that it was a nightmare come to trouble my sleep, but my limbs wouldn't move. I was fixed there like a statue of myself, unable to think, unable to feel, scarcely able to breathe. And then, somehow, Thyestes was staring into my face. I could see the hairs in his nostrils. I could smell his breath and see his teeth as he spoke. He had my thin arms gripped so tightly in his hands that I knew they must leave bruises there. I could see my mother's blood spattered on his clothes and chest. My teeth were chattering. I think my whole body must have been shaking. I could hear what he was saying and it made no sense to me. He was telling me that he and I were father and son and that my mother was also my sister. He insisted that he, not Atreus, was my true father, and we were both, therefore, monsters. A monstrous father embracing his monstrous son. My mother lay between us with my sword protruding from her stomach. I watched as he gripped it by the hilt and pulled out the blade with a soft puckering of sound in the silence of that place. A fresh spurt of blood burst out across the floor. I was staring at it when Thyestes grabbed me by the chin and fixed me with his gaze. He demanded to know what name they had given me, and when I gasped it out between my chattering teeth he said, "Well, Aegisthus, you are faced with the first and most important decision of your accursed young life. You must take back your sword and do one of two things with it. Either you can do what you came here to do and plunge it into my flesh, and this time I will not try to prevent you because you will be bringing an end to all my evil days. Or you can use it to kill the man who sent you here to murder me." He was staring so intently into my eyes that I could not look away from him and he must have divined the confusion of my thoughts because he said, "Be assured that Atreus is not your father." Then he gravely offered me the sword.'

Aegisthus stared into space remembering how cold he had felt in that moment. Cold and immensely powerful – a child given absolute power in a world in which the adults knew only how to hate each other. For a few seconds he had felt utterly free to choose. And then, only a moment later, he had known himself under a compulsion that left him with no choice at all. He saw Pelopia lying dead in her blood on the stone floor and Thyestes standing over her, and he knew that the three of them were caught in the trap of their terrible consanguinity. In a place prior to reason, older even than thought, he knew that the three of them were all one flesh; that they were an unholy family living and dying inside a trap that had been set for them by a malevolent fate.

'And there was no escape,' he said. 'I would do what my true father told me to do. I would return to Atreus with the bloody sword, claiming that I had done his will and murdered his brother Thyestes. And then, when his back was turned, perhaps in the very moment when he was making a thankful offering to the gods he worshipped, I would take that sword and drive it with all my strength up through his back and into his lungs and heart. And in so doing I would have fulfilled the Delphic oracle and avenged my father on his enemy.'

'And in that moment,' Clytaemnestra whispered urgently, 'tell me, what did you feel?'

Aegisthus looked up, aware suddenly of the almost sensual appetite with which she waited for his answer. 'Now I shall disappoint you,' he said, 'for the truth is that I felt very little. I think that by then I was beyond all feeling as I was beyond all thought.

Without understanding what was happening to me, I had become an instrument of fate as devoid of moral consciousness as was my sword itself. Perhaps I had given my whole being over to my sword, the sword that Thyestes had purchased with the intention of killing his brother all those years before. The sword he had held at his daughter's throat when he ravished her. The sword with which the mother of his child had killed herself that night. And the sword which I now thrust into the back of the man whom I once believed to be my father and who I now knew to be a greater monster than my true father had ever been. And I did it with no sense of triumph. Nor even with much in the way of fear; merely with the dull certainty that my misbegotten life had fulfilled the purpose for which it was created and it would not greatly matter if I died for it.'

'But you did not die,' Clytaemnestra smiled.

'No, I did not die. There were men in Mycenae who were still loyal to Thyestes, and others who blamed the crime of Atreus for all the evil fortune that had fallen on the city. When my father was released from his shackles and the news spread that Atreus was dead, these people quickly rallied to his cause. By daybreak Thyestes was King in Mycenae and I was honoured as his heir. Agamemnon and Menelaus went into hiding and were eventually smuggled out of the city by their friends. Had he been wiser, Thyestes would have hunted them down before they left, but I think he was troubled by the thought that they too might be his sons by Aerope, and he was reluctant to risk bringing the guilt of their deaths on his head. It was a mistake, of course, as he learned to his cost years later when they came to Mycenae with the Spartan army of King Tyndareus at their backs and took the city by treachery. It was my turn then to flee for my life.'

'But again,' Clytaemnestra said, 'you did not die.'

'No, it seems that the gods still had a use for me.'

But Clytaemnestra did not answer his smile. She said, 'Can you still believe in the gods after all you have suffered in this life?'

'It seems to me that there are two possibilities,' Aegisthus answered coolly. 'Either there are divine powers who see more deeply into things than we do and who shape our destinies in larger ways than we can conceive in order to work their justice in the world; or there is no meaning and no justice in our lives and we are merely the absurd creatures of our own appetites and ignorance. If I am honest with you, I have to say that I have no idea which of these versions of the world is truly the case. But in either dispensation I am content to follow my own will rather than bow to the will of any other man. And because it seems to me that if the gods do exist, it would be a foolish man who failed to honour them, I make my offerings to Artemis, as the divine incarnation of that savage power which I see at work in the world around me whichever way I turn my eyes.'

To his satisfaction Aegisthus saw the woman across from him nodding as he spoke. 'However,' he added smiling, 'I recognize that in so doing I may be worshipping nothing more than a ruthless drive for life inside myself. Is not that, after all, why you invited me here?'

'It is,' Clytaemnestra assented, content in the knowledge that she had found the perfect instrument of her own cold-minded passions.

Getting up from her couch, she crossed the marble floor to stand before him and took between her own hands the hand on which he wore the serpent ring that she had sent to him. 'Now come,' she whispered, lifting that hand and pressing it to her breast, 'let you and I cleave together as these serpents do. And I shall help you to have your justice as you shall help me to have mine.'

And in the cold stones that lay behind the painted plaster of the chamber she had made beautiful, all the ghosts of Mycenae were stirring as she spoke.

The Bitch's Tomb

Even as the Argive ships pushed out into the bay of Troy it became clear that Poseidon would grant them no easy passage home. The weather had darkened since the night of the earth-tremor. Blackish-grey clouds, bullied across the sky by a hard wind out of the east, had broken into rain, and many of the vessels were so laden with spoil that they began to ship water even before they broached the mouth of the Hellespont. Once out on the open sea, the wind gathered force and as ships tipped and yawed among the waves, men regretted that they had not followed the examples of Menelaus and Nestor and left Troy two days earlier. Soon they began to fear both for their treasure and their lives.

Odysseus had thought twice before putting out to sea that day; but he could smell lasting trouble on the wind and wanted to be away from Troy, so he decided to risk the crossing back to Argos rather than be kept landlocked on that desolate shore. Yet unlike Diomedes and Idomeneus, who chose to risk the direct crossing by way of Lemnos, Odysseus remained with Agamemnon's fleet as it hugged the coast between Imbros and the long peninsula of Thrace. The voyage home would certainly take longer by that route, but he hoped that a few additional days at sea might allow time for his troubled mind to settle once more. He was as haunted now by the dream that had come to him on the night of the tremor as he was by his memories of the slaughter in Troy. Once or twice he had found himself washing obsessively as though a tide of blood kept rising through his skin. At other times he trembled uncontrollably. More deeply than ever he yearned for Penelope's embrace, but he was convinced that she must recoil from the hot broil of anger, guilt and self-disgust still swirling inside him. So he shied from the thought of presenting himself before his wife, and kept to himself as much as possible, hoping that time might quieten the turmoil in his mind.

While his crew strained at the oar-benches under shortened sail, their captain stood at the stern, staring back at where thick smoke still rose from the ruins of the city. The conflagration had been so vast, and its heat so tremendous, that it had taken on the force and scale of a natural disaster; but there was nothing natural about that murky haze. A world was burning there and men had set fire to it. The smoke billowing upwards from the ruins across a livid sky seemed to reflect the darkness still burning in his mind. It sickened him to look at it.

But when he turned away he saw Queen Hecuba standing at the rigging with her silver-grey hair blowing about her face. She said, 'Do you think the gods will look with favour on your work, Odysseus of Ithaca?'

To the best of his knowledge this was the first coherent sentence the old woman had spoken since the murder of her daughter Polyxena. Nor had she eaten since the fall of the city and her once majestic features were scrawny and hollow now. She looked less like a queen than a mad woman such as could be seen hanging about temple courtyards, chanting prophecies and beseeching alms. Yet there was an unforgiving sanity in the accusation of her eyes.

'I do not presume to speak for the gods,' Odysseus answered.

'Then speak for yourself,' she demanded. 'Are you proud of what you've done?'

'I take pride in the courage of my friends,' he prevaricated.

'And if you were to come home,' she said, 'and find that your son had been murdered and your wife carried off into slavery – would you still take pride in what men such as these can do?'

Odysseus made the sign to ward off evil and turned his face away from her.

'Be careful of what you say, old woman, or I'll have you kept below decks where no one can hear you.'

Hecuba brushed the hair from her gaunt cheeks. 'You find the truth of things too painful? Then perhaps one day we will understand one another, you and I.'

She gazed back at the burning city again and winced as a twisting pillar of lurid smoke gushed skywards from the citadel of Ilium. For a moment the despair in her face was so intense that he thought she might pull herself up by the rigging and throw herself over the side. But Hecuba remained where she was, rising and falling with each lurch of the ship, watching Troy vanish in charred ruins and a smear of smoke. She began to sing then, a low, heart-stirring lament for the city and its exterminated world. Her knuckles whitened at the yards. The grief in her song lifted on the stiff breeze, carrying across the oar-benches for all to hear, and when the women cowering beneath the afterdeck saw that Odysseus could not bring himself to silence her, they too joined in the refrain.

So the ship passed on past Cape Sigeum out of the bay of Troy. The scarlet prow of *The Fair Return* dipped and climbed among the white-caps but with no hint of triumph in her progress or any sign of the joy that might have come from the thought of returning home. Even the coarsest man aboard seemed burdened by a doleful sense of the transience of things.

They had not been long at sea when the wind turned and it became ever harder to make way through the swell. Hours passed in a back-breaking, slow tussle against wind and waves. Odysseus knew that they would have to put in at some haven before nightfall but this coastline remained hostile terrain. Throughout the ten years of the war only Achilles had seen much success fighting along the Thracian shore, and plenty of men in the Argive ships nursed bad memories of hard-fought encounters in these parts. Queen Hecuba was herself the daughter of a Thracian king, and though many of her father's warriors had died fighting for Troy, many more of the most ferocious tribesmen in the known world remained to guard their homeland against Argive marauders. Yet the seas were too high to risk the rigours of this coastline by darkness when the ships would be little more to each other than an unstable constellation of oil-lamps flickering in the blackness of the Aegean night.

Then, in the late afternoon, the small pinnace that Agamemnon used for delivering messages throughout the fleet pulled up alongside *The Fair Return*. The herald Talthybius stood clutching the rigging with one hand while holding the other cupped at his mouth against the wind. 'The fleet can put in safely here on the Thracian Chersonese,' he shouted. 'King Polymnestor has declared an end to hostilities rather than risk what he thinks might be a full-scale invasion.'

'You're sure about this?' Odysseus shouted back.

'Absolutely. He's given the High King proof of his shift in loyalties. Signal your ships to follow you into shore. There's to be a feast tonight.'

The pinnace put its head about to approach the Locrian ships that were battling the swell further out towards Imbros. The helmsman pushed over the steering oar of *The Fair Return* to make for the shore and, having seen to the trimming of the sail, Odysseus went down to lend a hand at the oars. As he was settling himself at the bench he heard an anxious muttering and suppressed moans from the Trojan women under the afterdeck. He could make out nothing distinctly except two names – Polymnestor and Polydorus. Clearly the women had heard what Talthybius had said and the news was causing consternation among them. But then Odysseus was heaving on the oar and could hear nothing more above the creak of the rowlocks and the slap of the waves against the side of the ship.

★　★　★

By the time *The Fair Return* made landfall on the Thracian Chersonese, Agamemnon's Mycenaeans were already pitching their tents outside the fortified stronghold which was the hilltop citadel of King Polymnestor. The camp was only lightly guarded and the troops seemed relaxed enough, so Odysseus made his way to Agamemnon's tent to discover how this unexpectedly friendly welcome had come about.

'Panic,' Agamemnon answered, smiling, when he looked up from where his scribe was penning a brief despatch that would be carried by pigeon back to Clytaemnestra in Mycenae. 'The destruction of Troy has shaken everyone's nerves in these parts and our progress has been watched all along the coast. Polymnestor must have thought we were planning to launch an attack against him because he hadn't expected the fleet to come this way. And it turns out that he had a particular reason to fear my wrath.'

Irritated by the complacent smirk on Agamemnon's face, Odysseus wilfully declined to ask what that reason might be. He was remembering how this man had swollen like a bullfrog to receive the triumphant acclaim of the host outside Troy. He was remembering how the King of Men had dragged his own reluctant figure up before the Scaean Gate to share in that acclaim. He had no interest in yielding him further satisfactions.

Aware of the rebuff but refusing to be discomposed by it, Agamemnon pressed the lion stamp of his signet-ring into the seal of the missive and dismissed the scribe. 'Have you heard of Priam's youngest son Polydorus?' he asked.

Odysseus nodded. 'He was only a boy, wasn't he? Didn't he come out onto the field against his father's wishes and fall to the spear of Achilles?'

'That's what I thought too,' Agamemnon smiled. 'But it seems the Polydorus that Achilles killed was only one of Priam's bastards. He'd been given the name as cover for the real Polydorus who was Hecuba's youngest son and of the true blood. Priam sent the boy away from Troy early in the war so that his line didn't die out completely if the city fell. He's been living here in the court of Polymnestor and his Queen Iliona, who's one of Priam's daughters and sister to Polydorus.'

'So Polymnestor thought you'd come here to smoke him out?'

'Exactly; and when he saw the size of the fleet bearing down on his headland he decided the game wasn't worth the candle. So he did the job for me himself.'

'He intends to hand the boy over to you?'

'He's already done so. When he saw my ship approaching he pushed his body out to sea with a message attached to it explaining the situation.'

'So he's already dead.'

'Very dead.'

'And now we're all good friends?'

Agamemnon frowned at the sarcasm. 'Personally, I wouldn't trust this Thracian kingling as far as I could throw him. But he knows that the balance of power has shifted across the Aegean once and for all and he's looking for allies not for enemies. In the meantime we have a place to beach the ships till the wind changes. I don't expect any trouble from him.'

'How old was the boy?' Odysseus was thinking – as Hecuba had challenged him to do – about his own son, Telemachus.

'Twelve? Thirteen? All I know for sure is that there's no way he's going to grow up and come looking to avenge his father now. So that really is the last of Troy.'

'And what about Queen Iliona?'

'What about her?'

Odysseus sighed at the obtuseness. 'Are we to assume she was content to see her little brother murdered by her husband?'

'Who knows?' Agamemnon shrugged, increasingly annoyed by the Ithacan's refusal to share his pleasure. 'Perhaps she's just thanking her gods that she's better off than her wretched mother.'

'And Cassandra?' Odysseus pressed. 'Wasn't she the boy's sister too? What are her feelings about this?'

Agamemnon lost patience then. 'In the name of the gods, why do you always have to look on the black side of things? Can't you see we've struck lucky again? And the beauty of it is I had no more idea of Polydorus' existence than you did. So cheer up, you miserable Ithacan. We're going to dine at Polymnestor's expense tonight. I want you to come and get very drunk with the rest of us.'

But Odysseus was in no mood for drunken revelry. He was thinking that in some declivity of her pain, Queen Hecuba must have been sustained by the secret knowledge that, for all the grievous losses she had endured, one of her sons still survived, hidden away on this northern peninsula where the Argives would never find him. Now that son had been betrayed. Sooner or later she must learn that Polydorus was among the dead, murdered by his sworn protector, her own royal son-in-law, a Thracian kinsman. Odysseus could not conceive how even a mind and heart as strong as Hecuba's could withstand this final blow.

By the time he joined the feast that the Thracians had arranged for Agamemnon and his captains, the evening had already deteriorated into a rowdy binge over which Polymnestor presided with a canny, bibulous vigilance. A small, tubby man with a ginger moustache forking to either side of his narrow lips, he took pleasure in feeding titbits from the table to a gaudy parrot that was tethered by a golden chain to a perch at his side. The hall was clammy with heat from the huge fire blazing at the central hearth, and many slaves – whose pallid, greyish skins suggested they had been captured in some barbarian territory far to the north – were kept busy, serving the tables from the sides of beef and hog-meat turning on the spits, and pouring wine from amphorae to the mixing-bowls and thence to the goblets of the guests. Eager to be generous with his hospitality, the Thracian king seemed disappointed that Agamemnon remained more attentive to Cassandra, who sat beside him next to her sister Queen Iliona, than to the broad-hipped, half-naked dancing girls whose chains of silver baubles jangled as they rolled their bellies to the plangent sound of pipes and drums.

Having decided he would not remain long in that drunken company, Odysseus was already thinking of leaving when Polymnestor sought him out, demanding that he take more wine and asking to hear more of the strategy of the wooden horse by which all of King Priam's might had finally been destroyed. Repelled by his unctuous manner, Odysseus kept his answers terse, insisting that without the courage of his companions inside the horse his own ingenuity would have counted for nothing. But Polymnestor seemed determined to make a friend of him and would not be deterred.

The din of the revelry buzzed in Odysseus' ears. The smell of too many people crowded in a hot space assailed his nose. His eyes shifted between the rotten teeth in Polymnestor's mouth and the golden torque around his throat. Amid the heave of human carnality around him, his mind flashed back on images of the silent bodies of the Trojan dead. He heard himself saying, 'But weren't you and Priam kinsmen and friends?'

Evidently untroubled by the question, Polymnestor twisted his lips in a weary moue. He opened his hands as though to let something drop. 'The world changes, my friend,' he smiled. 'A man who fails to change with it is nothing.'

'And in such a world,' Odysseus asked, 'how shall a man know who to trust?'

A little ruffled by such seriousness on what was intended to be a light-hearted occasion, Polymnestor stroked his moustache with a heavily ringed finger. 'Ah, we are men of the world, you and I,' he said. 'We know that loyalty can be bought and sold. One need only keep an eye on the going price.'

Odysseus felt the sweat breaking at his brow. The hand holding his drinking-cup was trembling. With a stammered excuse that he was feeling ill, he turned away, leaving his host gaping after him as he pushed through the rowdy throng of men and women dancing round him, and out into the chilly air of the Thracian night.

The cloud-cover had broken, and a gibbous moon hung its

radiance across the turbulent sea. In the silence of the night Odysseus became conscious of a sound filling the channels of his ears of which he had not been conscious before, like a muffled alarm still ringing in an empty city. He had been standing alone for some time, trying to shake his head clear, half-afraid that he was losing his grip on his mind, when he heard a woman's voice behind him.

'Lord Odysseus?'

Turning, he saw Cassandra standing there. She was wearing a cloak draped over her head and shoulders against the night wind. A thin hand held the folds of cloth together at her throat.

She said, 'The entertainment is not to your taste?'

'Neither the entertainment nor the company.'

She stepped a little closer towards him. 'Then will you be patient with me for a moment? There is something I need to ask of you.'

Thinking that this strange young woman had never previously shown the least sign of humility in his presence, he said. 'There's nothing I could grant that you could not extract more easily from your new lord and master.'

'You are wrong,' she answered. 'This thing is in your power.'

Uneasily Odysseus said, 'What is it?'

'I have been talking with my sister Iliona. She has not seen our mother for many years and longs to do so. I have told her that Hecuba is held by you. I have also told her that, alone among the Argive generals, you have shown compassion for the sufferings of the captive women. It is Iliona's wish that you allow our mother to come to the palace so that we can grieve together for the death of Polydorus. I told her that I did not think that Odysseus would refuse this wish.'

Staring through the darkness at the pale, always enigmatic face of the woman across from him, he said, 'Hecuba doesn't yet know that her son is dead.'

'Then be merciful and let her daughters be the ones to tell her.'

'Am I to understand that Queen Iliona had no part in her brother's death?'

'You may understand,' Cassandra replied with alarming honesty, 'that she has as little love in her heart for Polymnestor as do I for Agamemnon.'

'And does Agamemnon know this?'

'The High King knows what he wishes to know.'

'Which may be less than is good for him?'

Cassandra merely shrugged beneath the linen cloak.

After a moment Odysseus said, 'Do you give me your word that the three of you will not conspire together against Agamemnon?'

'It was not Agamemnon who murdered Polydorus.'

'That doesn't answer my question.'

'If I were to give you my word, would you believe it?'

It was already evident to Odysseus that Cassandra had more in mind than a wake for a dead brother. From the unflinching way she held his gaze, he also saw that she was aware of his suspicions. Yet whenever this young woman spoke there was always a palpable air of truth about her as though her powers of prophecy had cursed her with a tongue that could not lie.

'Yes,' he heard himself answering, 'I believe that I would.'

'Then you have it,' she said.

As a matter of simple prudence, Odysseus informed Agamemnon the next day that he had given permission for Hecuba to leave his camp and visit her daughter Queen Iliona in the palace of King Polymnestor. Agamemnon confirmed that Cassandra had already spoken to him of this meeting and that he would do nothing to prevent it. Polymnestor had already suggested that they go hunting in the hills that day, and though he took little pleasure in the Thracian king's company, the expedition would make it possible for the meeting to take place without occasioning a bitter confrontation between Hecuba and her treacherous son-in-law. And so, later that day, accompanied by her serving-women, Hecuba made her way up the steep rise into the citadel.

But when Polymnestor returned from the hunt late that afternoon he found Hecuba waiting for him in his palace. Recovering quickly from his surprise, he stood before her, open-armed, his face a mask of grief and sympathy for all the misfortunes that had befallen her. Profuse with apologies that he had not sought her out sooner, he declared that he had only just learned from Agamemnon that she was held in the Argive camp by Odysseus. That strange fellow had said nothing of it at the previous night's feast or he would certainly have come at once to offer her his comfort and condolences. 'How to account for such calamities,' he lamented, 'except to say that we are all helpless before the will of the gods? Sometimes I wonder whether they deal with us so capriciously merely to make us revere them out of a simple fear of the unknown.'

Without allowing her eyes to settle on him, Hecuba nodded. 'There can be no comfort for my grief – though it has been some solace to know that Polydorus is in your safe keeping still.'

Polymnestor could only mirror her nodding for a moment, wondering what he would say if this half-crazed queen asked to see her son. Before he could think of a way to pre-empt the request, she was saying, 'I would dearly love to look on his face again but Iliona tells me that you wisely concealed him far upcountry when you saw the Argive fleet approach. The beast of Mycenae would not have let him live an hour longer if he had laid his foul hands on him.' Then she leaned her hawkish features forward, gripping his wrist. 'But as long as Polydorus lives,' she hissed, 'all is not over for us.'

'No,' he murmured uncertainly, 'while there is life there is always hope.'

'And you have the gold safe that we sent to you from Troy?'

'Yes, it's all quite safe in my treasury. The Argives know nothing of it.'

Again Hecuba nodded. 'I see that we chose well, Priam and I, when we sent our son to you as our forlorn hope. Few men could dissemble so. If we are patient, dear friend, our hour must surely come.'

Conscious of the pain in his wrist where her fingers gripped him like talons, Polymnestor dared not pull away. He looked down into her face and caught what he thought to be the glint of madness in her eyes. Was this indomitable old woman really still hoping that her last surviving son could mount a campaign against the might of Mycenae with the gold that Priam had shipped from Troy into his vaults? Yet after all she had endured it seemed only charitable to humour her in this last pathetic illusion.

'And when that hour comes,' he said, 'I shall be ready.'

Hecuba released his hand and glanced up at him so fiercely that he thought for a moment that she had seen through his deceit. But then it was as if the strength went out of her. She caught her breath as though to stifle the tears that might otherwise overwhelm her and said, 'Apart from my servants who are as helpless as myself, I am a woman alone in the world. Whether I wish to or not, I must now look for help. I have only you to turn to, Polymnestor.'

What was she going to ask of him? He stood uneasily, wondering now whether it might not be wiser to disentangle himself from this old woman and her desperate dreams. Let her face the stark truth of her circumstances as he had been forced to do once Troy had fallen and the Argive fleet sailed into his waters.

'There is more,' she said.

Despite his consternation, the man was astute enough to pick up the fervour of a silent message in her eyes. If he was prepared to hear, this woman might still have something to say that might prove to his advantage.

'More?'

Her gaze flitted around the chamber, making sure that she could not be overheard. Then it settled on his face again. 'More gold lies buried beneath the ruins of Troy. Buried where all the Argive army could not find it.'

After a moment Polymnestor said, 'King Priam was ever gifted with great foresight. But can this gold still be recovered?'

'I cannot do it. Not while I am held captive by Odysseus. And there is no one left alive in Troy that I can trust.'

Polymnestor allowed a further deferential silence to pass before saying, 'You know that I have always stood at your service.'

'I know it, and may the gods reward you as you deserve. But where there is gold there is also temptation. If I were to tell you how it might be found, do you swear that you would use it only to further my son's righteous cause?'

'As your son lives,' said Polymnestor, 'I so swear it.'

He saw a fierce little smile of gratitude cross Hecuba's face, a smile that might have shrivelled the heart of a more scrupulous man. She said, 'I knew that I could rely on you to respond as I thought.' Then she looked away and began to finger the long strands of her silver-grey hair and chew at her lower lip so that he began to wonder if her wits had gone astray at this most critical of moments.

'This treasure must be buried in a truly secret place,' he said.

'It is. And all who placed it there are dead.'

'Then how shall it be recovered?'

The lines of Hecuba's gaunt features wrinkled in a cunning smile. 'There is a map, a clay tablet inscribed by Priam's own hand. It shows precisely where the treasure lies – on the site where the Temple of Athena once stood. Even among the ruins, it can easily be found with the guidance of this map.'

Polymnestor lowered his own voice to a whisper as he said, 'Then it should be kept securely. Do you have it with you?'

Frowning, she shook her head. 'Had Odysseus seen me leaving the camp with it, he would certainly have taken it from me. And the man is ingenious enough to work out its significance. No, I dared not risk it.'

Suppressing his excitement, Polymnestor said, 'But surely it should be put beyond his reach as soon as possible? Let me send for it.'

'I will deliver it only into your hands,' Hecuba said. 'I trust no one else.'

'I understand.' He fingered his moustache. 'Then I must find some pretext to come to your tent.'

'But if Odysseus sees you there he is sure to suspect something.'

'Then I must come unannounced,' he frowned, 'and under cover of darkness.'

Hecuba clutched at his wrist again. 'The women's pavilion stands apart from those of the men. It is easily found. If you come there by dark no one will see you carry the map away. Dare you do this thing for me?'

'It shall be done tonight.'

'And you must come alone,' Hecuba urged.

Immediately she sensed him stiffen. He was about to demur but she closed her other hand over the one that gripped his wrist. 'We cannot allow anyone else to guess at this secret.' Her voice was urgent, her harrowed eyes were all appeal. 'Where the prize is so great, only kinsmen are to be trusted . . . and I confess to you, even that comes hard.'

'Have I not kept faith with you all these years?' he reassured her. 'Once this gold is secured we shall have the means to see that Troy rises again.'

'With my son on the throne,' she pressed. 'Polydorus is the rightful heir to Troy. Remember you are sworn to his service.'

'Rest assured, madam, this gold will be as safe with me as your son has been.'

'Then I see you swear truly,' Hecuba said and released his hand.

The first that Odysseus knew of the consequences of this encounter was a terrible screaming in the night. Reaching for his sword, he rushed from his tent. The moon was still big and radiant in the night. By the milky light it cast across his camp, he saw a small hunched figure shrinking away from him with grey hair blowing about her face. A sound issued from her lips but whether the gasps were of anguish or of crazy laughter he would have been hard-pressed to say. The canopy of the women's pavilion flapped in the night breeze at her back. It was from there that the sound of screaming came.

'Hecuba,' Odysseus demanded as other men appeared around him, 'what is it? Has someone assaulted you?'

But the old woman did not answer him. She merely stood there in the gloom, looking down in fascination at whatever it was she clutched in her hands. Sinon came up beside Odysseus holding a torch he had lit from the camp-fire. In the same moment another figure staggered into the moonlight out of the women's tent. He was holding a hand across his face, screaming for help and crying out that the bitch had blinded him. When the man lowered the hand to help feel his way, Odysseus saw that his face was streaming with blood. Yet he recognized the forked moustache and portly figure of Polymnestor.

The Thracian king stumbled over a guy-rope and fell to the ground where he lay in torment, shrieking curses at the night. Quickly Odysseus crossed to help him and winced at the hideous sight that confronted him when Polymnestor looked up in the glare from Sinon's torch. Above the clotted strands of facial hair, the eye-sockets were two craters rimmed with bloody flesh and fringed with broken veins. He could hear Hecuba howling in the night behind him – quick, raucous yelps of triumph or of horror – who knew which? – bayed hoarsely upwards at the moon. He knew then what it was that she held in her hands.

More men were gathering round him. Then he heard the voice of Agamemnon demanding to know what all this commotion was. Out of the corner of his eye Odysseus saw Hecuba's serving-women cowering together in the shadows of the tent and guessed that their combined strength must have pinned the Thracian King to the ground while, for the want of any more lethal weapon, their grief-crazed mistress had used her bare hands to gouge out his eyes.

Leaving Polymnestor whimpering under the ministrations of a physician, Odysseus pulled away, feeling his gorge rise. But Agamemnon called him back, demanding to know how this thing had been allowed to happen.

'It happened because we started a war, 'Odysseus answered bitterly. 'I doubt now that there can ever be an end to it.'

'The war is over and won,' Agamemnon snapped back. 'Pull yourself together, and get that woman silenced and bound before she does more harm.'

But as the two men turned to look at her, Hecuba disappeared in the gloom between the tents, making for the ships. Calling Sinon to join him, Odysseus ran after her scurrying figure. He had not gone more than a few yards when he slipped on something in the rough grass under his feet. Looking down, he saw the sole of his foot smeared with the jelly of one of Polymnestor's eyes.

Odysseus was retching as Sinon caught up with him. By the time the two men arrived at the ships, Hecuba had already clambered aboard the nearest vessel, which happened to be *The Fair Return*. She stood with her hand at the rigging, staring up at the moon, singing the lament for Troy that had come to her as they sailed away from the burning city. Against the plunge of the breakers and the hoarse rattle of the shingle racing back into the sea, her voice was little more than a torn and ragged muttering to the night.

'The woman's out of her mind,' Sinon whispered.

'And has been, I think, for longer than we know.'

'What are we going to do?'

'I don't know.'

Sinon said, 'The gods have done their worst with her.'

Odysseus looked at him with narrowed eyes. 'You blame the gods for this?'

Sinon shrugged. 'We are always in their hands.'

Before Odysseus could answer, a change came over Hecuba's voice. At first he thought that the Queen was in tears, overwhelmed by the pressure of her grief, but then he recognized the guttural, panting breaths cracking from her throat as a resumption of the barely human noise she had been making earlier.

'Listen to her,' Sinon whispered in horrified awe.

'Hecuba!' Odysseus called out to whatever might remain of a human soul inside her anguished frame. But for all the notice she took, he might as well have been shouting at a disobedient dog. Hecuba had withdrawn to a region so remote from human reach that she had no use left for language. Only the moon, radiant and cold, commanded her attention. Clutching the rigging in blood-stained hands, she pulled herself up from the deck onto the side of the ship and began to climb towards the masthead. Again Odysseus called out her name. Again, if she heard him at all, she ignored him. Cursing that in his desire to make a quick getaway he had ordered that the mast be left unstepped, he watched her clamber upwards with an agility that belied the frailty of her years.

'The crazy bitch is trying to reach the moon,' Sinon said.

And spoke Odysseus's own thought.

Moments later she was at the masthead, her silver hair blowing like a banner in the breeze, one hand outstretched as though, were she to lean just a few inches further into space, she might have that bright shell in her grasp for ever. Stars glittered among the clouds and went dark again. The surf plunged and boomed against the strand. Queen Hecuba, wife of Priam, First Lady of royal Troy, and among the most tragic women ever to dignify the earth, was still barking like a tethered dog when her fingers lost her grip on the mast and she plummeted – a ragged spectre in the moonlight – to the ship's deck thirty feet below.

Odysseus commanded that Hecuba's remains be buried beneath a funerary mound on a headland of the peninsula that forms the northern shore of the Hellespont across the water from Troy. Ever afterwards the place was known by the name that Sinon gave it – Cynossema, the Bitch's Tomb.

Some days later, the fleet was beating along the Thracian shore past the tribal lands of the Cicones when Sinon's ship, *The Jolly Dolphin,* struck a rock on a shoal concealed beneath the swell and sprang a larboard strake.

Heavily burdened with loot, the vessel was already riding low among the waves. Now she was shipping so much water that she must surely sink unless they could raise the damaged timber above the water-line. Cursing his ill-luck, Sinon watched from the helm as his crew frantically bailed with skins, jars and helmets – whatever they could find. Most of those men were as little able to swim as he was himself and he had quickly signalled for aid, but the sluggish progress of his over-laden ship had left him some distance behind the main body of the fleet. He could see no choice now but to start dumping his precious cargo into the sea.

The Fair Return had immediately put about in speedy answer to the signal. She hove alongside the *Dolphin* just in time for Odysseus to see a golden effigy of Aphrodite topple over the side and plunge beneath the waves head-first in a dispiriting inversion of the manner of her ocean birth. A few minutes later it became clear that the damaged vessel had been saved but only by dint of shedding the vast bulk of her cargo. It was equally clear that she had no hope of coping with heavy seas without first putting in for repairs. But the swell was too high to risk making a run for the distant island of Samothrace, and when Odysseus looked towards the nearer mainland shore, he could make out the Ciconian city of Ismarus perched on its mountain. The Cicones had always been staunch allies of Troy. Were he to leave Sinon's ship unsupported on that hostile coast, his cousin and crew would soon be cut down.

Odysseus cursed beneath his breath. Almost from the first moment he had climbed out of the belly of the horse, everything seemed to have gone wrong for him. He wanted nothing more now than to reach Ithaca as soon as possible, yet with every day that passed, his homeland seemed to recede into a hazy region of serenity and peace from which he might be forever excluded. The ravages of the war had left him in command of only twelve ships – a mere fifth of the sixty he had led out of the Ionian Islands ten years before. Many of his friends were dead. The ghost of Hecuba seemed to haunt his ship. And now it seemed he was opposed by the unpredictable power of Poseidon himself.

Signalling to his other ships to follow, Odysseus ordered his helmsman Baius to put the prow about, and made for the Thracian shore with *The Jolly Dolphin* limping behind. Meanwhile, several miles away by now and unconcerned over the mishap, the rest of the Argive fleet vanished into the afternoon mist.

They made landfall in a sheltered cove along the coast from Ismarus. Odysseus felt confident that the Ithacan force was strong enough to deter anything other than a large and well-organized attack, but they would be holed up there for at least another day before the damage was repaired, so he sent out scouts to assess the strength of any likely opposition. Meanwhile, bored and restless, the other crews grumbled resentfully when Sinon declared that it was only just that they should give up a portion of their booty to compensate his crew for their loss.

Their fellow Ithacans grudgingly assented on condition that everyone else agreed to do the same, but the men of Dulichion and Zacynthos grew vociferous in their resistance to the idea. Sinon's hoard had not been lost as a result of their faulty seamanship, so why should they be made to pay for it? Old rivalries and grudges quickly flared. As insults flew, Odysseus was beginning to worry that things must come to blows when one of the scouts returned, sent back with the report that they had found Ismarus surprisingly ill-defended.

'There's our answer then,' said Meges, leader of the Dulichians. 'Let Sinon's men lead us in a surprise attack and he can load his ship with Thracian gold.'

'It's not worth the risk,' Odysseus demurred. 'There's enough in our holds to make us all rich for life. We should make for home with what we have.'

The more sober of his followers agreed but Sinon was not among them. 'I need to salvage something from this bloody war,' he insisted, 'or ten years of misery will have gone for nothing.'

'They will have gone for less,' Odysseus said, 'if you end up skewered on a Ciconian spear.'

'I'll take my chances,' his cousin countered. 'Who will back me?'

Among the survivors of the war were a hard-bitten bunch of men who had grown so inured to the exertions of fighting that they were left fractious and ill-at-ease by the onset of peace. Enough of them raised their hands to leave the rest feeling paltry.

'We were all pirates before we were warriors,' Meges grinned, 'and I've heard that Ismarian wine is among the best there is. I look forward to trying it.'

When his Dulichian followers nodded along with him, it was clear that Sinon had his raiding-party.

They fell on Ismarus after dark while most of the unsuspecting citizens were dining. Odysseus had insisted that there should be no indiscriminate slaughter and this time there was no one to countermand him. But those among the Cicones who had time to reach for their weapons mounted a stiff resistance and many of them had to be killed before the others surrendered. Shocked and despondent, the disarmed men looked on as their palace and temples were stripped of their treasures. A band of Dulichians discovered a vast wine-cellar beneath the citadel and many amphorae of the best local vintage were loaded on to the requisitioned ox-wagons with all the gold, silver, copper and bronze that could be quickly gathered. Only a few hours after the raid had begun, and having taken no losses, the elated looters were back in the cove getting very drunk.

That might have been the end of it had not two of the outraged citizens of Ismarus ridden throughout the night stirring up support from the neighbouring cities, towns and villages. Early the next day, when the drunken raiders were barely coming to their senses again, they found themselves confronted by a superior force of Ciconian warriors gathered on the cliff-top above them.

Odysseus and his followers would almost certainly have been wiped out if the narrowness of the cliff-paths had not prevented their enemies from bringing their full force against them in a single attack. Even so, the top-knotted Ciconians fell on them in numbers. Their shouts and ululations panicked the long-horned oxen that had dragged the loaded wagons to the cove, and the Ithacans were caught up in a desperate skirmish across the strand as they tried to cover the retreat to the ships.

With his unseaworthy vessel still propped on the beach, Sinon died in that fight as did most of his crew. Meges was among those trampled beneath the hooves of the terrified long-horns. The black skin of Odysseus' herald Eurybates was torn into a vivid gash where a slingshot grazed his brow. Other men were brought down by archers as they scrambled aboard their ships. Odysseus himself was lucky to escape with his life when a brawny axe-wielding barbarian bore down on him in the fray. A youngster called Elpenor who had slept aboard *The Fair Return* that night saw the ruffian coming and let fly an arrow that pierced his lung before the axe could fall.

Somehow the Argives managed to run their ships out into the sea but it soon became clear that every crew was depleted by losses. As his own vessel rose on the heavy swell, Odysseus looked back from where he strained at his oar and saw the Cicones finishing off the wounded. Further along the beach others were reclaiming the pile of spoil that lay shining in a patch of sunlight near to where the fractured belly of *The Jolly Dolphin* lay careened on the strand. Then the scarlet prow of *The Fair Return* plunged into a trough and when it rose again the sunlight had faded from the beach.

Out across the sea, dense thunderheads rose black against the sky. Odysseus sensed their menace in the change of the light and the smell of the wind. The ship rolled among green breakers. Seabirds canted along the channels of the air. Around him, dismayed by the abrupt alteration in their fortunes, men gasped and groaned. Odysseus tried to fix his mind on the image of his

158

wife Penelope waiting for him at home on Ithaca; but with each
pull on the oar he felt himself drawn deeper into Poseidon's grip,
and deeper still into despair.

Cassandra

A knocking at the door of her bed-chamber woke Clytaemnestra from her sleep. Cautioning Aegisthus to lie still and be silent, she left the bed, crossed to the door, opened it, and listened as, in a voice trembling with excitement and apprehension, Marpessa, the trusted old beldame who aided the furtive comings and goings of Aegisthus, broke the news.

Aware of the sudden agitation of her heart, Clytaemnestra said, 'There can be no mistake?'

'I had it directly from the watchman,' Marpessa answered. 'The beacon fire was lit on Mount Arachne less than an hour ago. I came to wake you straight away.'

Clytaemnestra stood quite still in the night. After all the uncertain days of waiting and scheming, time was accelerating round her. Impossible at this hour, at this news, to sustain the studied calm that was her customary cold manner. Once again her heart became a cockpit of emotions. She gripped Marpessa in a fierce embrace, unable to repress the surge of elation that came with the news that the Argive host had triumphed in the greatest war the world had ever seen. How many hours had she and Agamemnon spent planning for this victory – prising the warlords of Argos out of their comfortable lives, requisitioning the ships, haggling over the price of supplies, making sure that the troops were well-armed, dealing with the countless logistical problems thrown up by the unprecedented task of moving a hundred thousand men from one side of the Aegean to the other? And there were so many setbacks, defeats and disappointments across the years that there had been times when the whole enterprise felt futile and absurd, a hubristic fantasy of two ambitious minds. Then a catastrophic storm had blown the fleet back to Aulis, and with that had come the atrocity of her daughter's death. Later Achilles had been slain, and Ajax too had died among countless lesser losses. Yet despite everything, Agamemnon had won through. The unbreachable walls of Troy were breached. Priam must be dead already, and the richest city in Asia looted and in flames. It was impossible, utterly impossible, for her heart not to sway with exhilaration at the titanic scale of what had been achieved!

Yet since the day that Aegisthus had come at her bidding to Mycenae, the prospect of Agamemnon returning to her bed in triumph had become more loathsome to her mind and senses than it had ever been. Whatever else he might be, he remained the slayer of her children still. There were crimes on his head that could never be forgiven. So along with the excitement came an almost breathless trepidation at the thought of what she planned to do.

Through an invisible effort of the will, Clytaemnestra stilled the dark elation in her heart. 'Very well, Marpessa,' she said quietly as though the woman had just informed her of some minor success in the domestic arrangements of the palace. 'This news is good. But return to your bed now. There will be time enough to celebrate tomorrow.'

Wondering once more at the strange implacability of the mistress she served, Marpessa nodded and turned away. Clytaemnestra lifted the oil-lamp from the sconce by the door and crossed back through into her bed-chamber where Aegisthus was sitting up against the pillows with a wry smile on his face.

'You heard?' she said.

'The Lion of Mycenae is Lord of Asia at last.'

'For the moment – unless he lingers too long and the Hittite legions push him back into the sea.'

'He must have received your warning by now.'

'No acknowledgement has come. We cannot yet be sure.'

Aegisthus smiled, pulling back the covers for her. 'Not that it makes a great deal of difference. Either way, he's a dead man.'

'It makes a great deal of difference. I want him to bring home the treasure of Troy before he crosses to the Land of Shades.' Clytaemnestra put down the lamp but she did not yet return to the bed. 'How long do you think it will take him to get back to Mycenae?'

'That rather depends on how much time they spend arguing over the spoils. And then there's the weather, of course. The seas are running high on this side of the Aegean and the wind is out of the east, so conditions are not likely to be any better over there and may be worse. I would guess we have at least a week to wait. Probably rather longer.' Aegisthus lay down in the bed again with his hands crossed beneath his head. 'I'm afraid it's going to be a nerve-racking time.'

Gathering a shawl about her shoulders. Clytaemnestra sat down beside him, her eyes narrowing in thought. 'We should send the children away tomorrow,' she decided. 'Helen's girl must go back to Sparta to await the return of Menelaus. I shall put Orestes and Electra in the charge of old Podargus at Midea until things have settled down here in Mycenae.'

'The boy will be difficult,' Aegisthus said. 'He's sure to want to witness his father's triumph.'

'Orestes will do as I tell him.'

'Which is more than I can say. He grows more insubordinate every day.'

Though she felt the heat rising to her throat, Clytaemnestra kept her voice calm. 'He's a tethered bull-calf,' she said. 'He's young, and frustrated that he's missing the war. Be patient with him. Orestes has no great love for his father. He'll come round well enough in time.'

Glancing away, Aegisthus said, 'I wish I could share your confidence.'

'Trust me,' she answered. 'I know my son.'

'Even though you see so little of him?'

When Clytaemnestra stirred impatiently, Aegisthus added, 'You should listen to me. Orestes is a little too full of himself. Just because his voice has broken he thinks he's already a man. And he's rather too close to the sons of people we have no reason to trust. I'm thinking in particular of young Pylades.'

'Pylades will shortly be recalled to Phocis by his father. I have already seen to that. And Orestes will be kept well apart from him in Midea.' She looked down at the angular cheekbones and deep-set, kinetic eyes of the man lying next to her. 'You should be easier with my son,' she said. 'Make allowances for him. Show a little more patience and be his friend.'

Drawing a deep breath, Aegisthus nodded his assent, though privately he considered that, for all the stern control she exhibited, Clytaemnestra's feelings were still too raw and protective where her children were concerned. Nor were they always realistic. There were things he might tell her if he chose, but they would only arouse an anger he had already learned to fear and further increase the invidiousness of his position; so he was reluctant to press the issue of Orestes any further at this time. In any case, there were influential figures at large inside Mycenae who presented a more immediate threat to the success of their plans than did Agamemnon's moody son. With Orestes gone from the city it would be easier to concentrate his mind on dealing with them.

'We should decide,' he said, 'when to make our move against Idas and that tiresome old fool Doricleus.'

Clytaemnestra rested the long fingers of one hand on her lover's shoulder. 'Calm yourself. Everything is in place. We've discussed this already. If we act too soon we'll alert Agamemnon's supporters in Tiryns and elsewhere.'

'And if we leave it too late one or other of them is sure to inform him that all is not as he thinks in Mycenae.'

'The timing will be exact.' There was a hint of impatience in Clytaemnestra's voice. 'Idas and Doricleus are watched. There's no reason why they should suspect that anything is wrong; and I'm quite sure that Agamemnon will give plenty of notice of his arrival so that I can arrange the kind of triumph he expects.' Lightening her tone a little, she added, 'We can leave him to determine the pace of events without knowing what he's doing.'

But she sensed that this unexpected ratcheting of the tension between them had left the man lying next to her more anxious than herself. Clytaemnestra moved further down into the bed to caress his hairless chest. 'Agamemnon is no more than a stone in my shoe,' she smiled. 'And Mycenae is ours already. Come, be easy on yourself. Take me in your arms. Make love to me.'

Far across the Aegean, Agamemnon watched *The Fair Return* go about and sail to the aid of Sinon's stricken vessel, but he had no intention of slowing his own progress along the Thracian shore. There were many reasons why he wanted to get back to Mycenae quickly now and that grisly business on the Chersonese had delayed him long enough. With the seas already running high and dirtier weather threatening from the east, he was anxious to make landfall as far west as he could before darkness fell. At the very least, he might put in on Thasos. With luck he might even find shelter for the night in the lee of Mount Athos.

When he turned to gaze ahead he saw Cassandra standing at the prow of the ship where the wind blew through her hair and spindrift softly broke against her face. Since her mother's death she had withdrawn into long elusive silences that would have troubled him more if the strength of their improbable alliance had much depended on the power of words. As it was, Agamemnon made allowances for her grief and told himself that she would soon grow warm at his side again when she heard him lauded by the adoration of the crowds.

He recalled the image of Cassandra weeping with her sister Iliona beside their mother's funeral mound as the final offerings were made. A cold wind had sliced out of the north, tugging at their robes and blowing smoke into their eyes. At the foot of the cliff, wave after wave smashed against the rock-face, each shaking the air with the force of its impact and falling back with a thunderous detonation. Seabirds clamoured overhead. With the wind thudding and sucking about her ears, Iliona shivered at her sister's side, venting her grief but, as yet, a mere novice – as Cassandra was not – in the mysteries of pain.

To avoid further trouble, Agamemnon had insisted that the serving-women who had helped Hecuba with the blinding of Polymnestor should be put to the sword. So with the possible exception of that increasingly strange fellow Odysseus, it had seemed to him that of all the people assembled on the bare headland, the two sisters were alone in mourning the queen's bleak death.

Again, standing at the stern of his flagship, Agamemnon stamped his feet against the cold. Remembering how discomfited he'd been by the sullen stare of Polymnestor's sons, he was wondering whether he should have finished them off lest one day they come to Mycenae with vengeance on their minds. But it was their crazy grandmother who had blinded their father, not he, and he wanted as little as possible to do with the whole unchancy affair. The sooner this accursed Thracian shore was at his back, the happier he would be.

Meanwhile, if truth were told, he was feeling damnably lonely. Menelaus was gone, banished somewhere over the eastern horizon, and the brothers might never see each other again. Grown gloomy and lugubrious since his son Antilochus had been killed only days before the city fell, garrulous old Nestor had sailed from Troy on the same day. Odysseus was now delayed in Thrace by the damage to Sinon's ship and was, in any case, no good company these days. Meanwhile Diomedes and Idomeneus had opted for a swifter route home, sailing southwards along the Asian coast before striking out for Argos and Crete.

It seemed that with the final triumph over Troy had come the breaking of the always uneasy Argive fellowship. Worse still, for all the treasure in the bellies of his ships, a curious, dispiriting emptiness had entered Agamemnon's heart. It baffled comprehension. Was he not now the most famous, powerful and wealthy monarch in the entire western world? Had he not led the largest army ever raised to the most complete of victories? He had achieved everything he had set out to do and thereby made himself into something closer to a god than to a mere mortal man. Was his name not immortal now? Heracles and Jason and Theseus had been great heroes in their day, but their day was done and this was the time of Agamemnon, Lion of Mycenae, Sacker of Cities, King of Men. Bards would sing of his deeds for ever. All of this was true and indisputable. Then why this sense of vacancy, as though his soul went hungry still? And how was it that he could find no consolation for that nameless deficiency except in the arms of Cassandra? The thought of it both alarmed and excited him, and all the more so because she had rebuffed his recent advances as though her pain was physical.

He was well aware that his men both wondered at the power the Trojan woman exercised over his moods and were dismayed by it, but none among them dared to speak of it within his hearing, and Agamemnon had taken to keeping his own counsel these days.

Meanwhile with every sea-mile that passed beneath the keel Cassandra's world was changing round her. As a princess of Troy she had rarely strayed outside the palace or the temple precinct. The air she breathed there was closeted within painted walls, heady with incense and the perfume of cut flowers. She had always been a child of the city, so when she first stepped aboard Agamemnon's ship, her heart had quailed at the prospect of a long exposure to the turbulent emptiness of sea and sky. She feared that her mind might dissolve in those volatile, windy spaces, for her prophetic spirit depended on her contact with the earth, and with such knowledge gone from her, what was she but a helpless woman like all the others who had been carried away from Troy to serve these coarse new masters with the labour of their flesh?

Her terror increased when they made landfall on the Thracian Chersonese and she realised that there were forces at work there that she had not foreseen. No prophetic pictures had prepared her mind for the horror of watching the murdered body of her brother Polydorus fetched up out of the sea. So she had stared at that poor corpse lying pallid and sodden on the deck of the ship, and knew herself overwhelmed less by grief for a brother she had hardly known than by the fear that her gift had left her forever.

It was her mother who had put her panicking spirit back inside her skin, for once Hecuba had accepted this latest and, as it turned out, final loss, a resolute calm had settled over her like a snow-field. All the women around her were awestruck by the change. The Trojan Queen was less a person now than an elemental force pursuing the line of least resistance as she set out to fulfil her own inexorable purposes. And as handmaid to the vengeful Fury that possessed her mother's soul, Cassandra had done everything that she was told to do. Strength had come with obedience. But she had known from the first that, one way or another, her mother must die for this. And she knew too that the choice to die was the only real freedom left to either of them now.

So she had come away from Cynossema with her clarity of mind restored. In spirit she already belonged to death, so there could be, she believed, nothing left in life to fear. Once she set foot on the earth again, her powers would return and she would be told exactly what the god required of her.

The tempest that struck as *The Fair Return* pulled away from the land of the Cicones was the worst the Aegean Sea had endured for years. In a tumult far more violent than the storm that had driven the Argive fleet back to Aulis a year earlier, bolt after bolt of lightning seared the sky, setting the spars alight so that the struck ships combusted like torches of oily tow. Awash among the billows, they foundered under a black sky thick with rain and loud with thunder. Men burned and drowned. Ships sank, taking their treasure to the bottom with them. By the time the seas subsided four days later, few of the surviving vessels were still in sight of one another, and fewer still knew where they were. Meanwhile, Poseidon and Athena had looked on with satisfaction.

Agamemnon was luckier than most of his fleet. Having a stronger ship and more oars at his command, he had made good headway since leaving Thrace and was able to take shelter in the lee of Mount Athos before the storm broke.

He fretted impatiently there but at least his weary oarsmen could rest rather than wasting their strength against the swell. But by the time his ship approached the dangerous promontory of Caphareus at the southernmost tip of Euboea he had begun to comprehend the full scale of the damage wreaked by the storm. All along the coast of Euboea smashed carcases of ships lay propped among the rocks. The waves were littered with wreckage and corpses, one of which lay floating on its back with an ankle tangled in the rigging of a spar. Though the flesh was puffy and discoloured, the features were still recognizable as those of Aias the Locrian, the man who had tried to ravish Cassandra as she clung to the Palladium in the temple of Athena at Troy. When one of the crew asked whether they should haul the body in and take it back to Locris for burial, Agamemnon merely scowled and shook his head. 'Divine Athena has taken her vengeance for his impiety,' he said. 'It would be unlucky to interfere.'

In any case, he had larger troubles on his mind. By the time they had doubled the cape he had counted the wreckage of at least sixty ships, and who knew how many more might have sunk without trace? He was appalled by the losses, and amazed by them too. Hadn't that brilliant young schemer Palamedes made sure that all the dangerous rocks and shoals of Euboea were marked by beacons? So how was it that so many ships had been driven aground?

With suspicions darkening his mind, Agamemnon considered

putting in at Eretria to demand an explanation of King Nauplius, but there would be time enough for that once he had disembarked at Aulis. Meanwhile his mind was fixed on the violent events more than a hundred miles to the north in Thessaly. Before he could allow his troops to disperse he needed to know whether or not they were urgently needed to halt the Dorian invasion.

As soon as he had docked at Aulis, he despatched Talthybius to Mycenae with instructions for the preparation of his triumphal return; then he summoned a council of the Boeotian and Locrian barons who had remained in Argos throughout the war. His intention was to gather as much information as he could about the struggle to throw back the Dorian invaders. In particular he wanted to find out whether it was truly the case that these barbarians were equipped with stronger weapons than any his own forces could command.

Almost all the news he received was bad. Neoptolemus and his Myrmidons had arrived too late to lift the siege of Iolcus, which was now firmly under Dorian control. Fortunately, Peleus had contrived to escape by sea as the city fell. Old and lame as he was, he had begun to organize a campaign of resistance to further incursions, and his depleted troops were greatly heartened by the return of the Myrmidons. Though the situation remained confused, as far as everyone knew, he and Neoptolemus were still holding the line in southern Thessaly.

Yet the mood among the Locrian contingent in Aulis was apprehensive. Their land would be the next to fall if the invasion was not halted and they were alarmed by many reports of the way bronze swords shattered against iron helmets and quickly broke in hand-to-hand fighting against iron blades. At the moment only the leaders of the Dorians were equipped with such invincible armour, but if the smiths forged enough of this weaponry to arm the entire Dorian horde then it could only be a question of time before all Argos fell.

'If they can make such weapons,' Agamemnon declared, 'then so can we.'

When he was reminded that the Argive smiths did not yet understand the magical processes by which iron was made, he demanded to know why no effort had been made to capture a Dorian smith and torment the secret out of him.

'That's easier said than done,' an old Locrian baron answered him. 'Their forges are behind their lines, far to the north of the fighting, and every smith who knows the secret is hamstrung to prevent him wandering off and selling his knowledge.'

'So at the end of the day we're fighting against cripples!' Agamemnon blustered.

'Yes,' the Locrian answered, 'but cripples who know how to make men of iron.'

Agamemnon came away from the council angry and frustrated. When he had first sailed from Aulis ten years earlier he had left behind him a strong, peaceful and united empire. With Priam defeated and his line extinct, only Hattusilis, Emperor of the Hittites, could compare with the Lion of Mycenae for strength and power, and his interests lay far to the east. Everything, therefore, should have been right with the world. Jubilation and acclaim should have been waiting for him here in Aulis. He should have found himself surrounded by crowds of dancing women and children, throwing flowers and singing paeans, not this worried bunch of old men muttering of trouble in the north. But the Dorians were clearly a formidable new foe. It couldn't be long before Neoptolemus called for his support in the struggle to keep them at bay; yet many of his own best fighting men had died under the walls of Troy and only the gods knew how many more had drowned in the storm. When the rest of his army got back home it would be in no mood for further fighting. Nor could Agamemnon be sure that, when all the losses were accounted for, there would be enough profit left from the war at Troy to finance another distant campaign.

In any case, he would have his hands full closer to home. With Menelaus banished, Sparta must be quickly placed in safe hands. Only trouble could be expected out of Euboea, and whichever of the sons of Theseus replaced Menestheus on the throne of Athens, Agamemnon now doubted that he could rely either on Acamas or Demophon for much support. They had not forgotten that Attica had been mighty in their father's time. Were Agamemnon to move his own forces northwards against the Dorians, Mycenae could soon be under threat at his rear. And somewhere amidst all this unanticipated turmoil, Aegisthus was still on the loose, harbouring his hatred for the sons of Atreus, eager to avenge his own father's death and to seize the Lion Throne for himself.

Agamemnon's anger wilted into gloom. He wanted Cassandra and the comfort of brief oblivion he had found in her embrace in the nights before the Thracian Chersonese. Yet even as the desire rose inside him, he recalled with a lurch of the heart, that there could only be more trouble when Clytaemnestra learned of her existence. The prospect of that imminent collision further darkened his mind.

The herald Talthybius travelled with as much speed as he could make along the muddy Isthmus road to Mycenae, breaking his journey for the night at a friend's house in a small town where men were shouting over a cock-fight in the square. Neleus had once been a herald himself, in service first to King Atreus, and then later, as a matter of expediency, to the usurper Thyestes; but he was among the early defectors to the cause of the Atreides when Agamemnon was fighting to regain the throne, and had been rewarded with a comfortable retirement in this farmhouse looking out across the Gulf of Corinth. These days he took more interest in tending his vines and groves than in the machinations of courtly life, but he had an ear for gossip and it was through him that Talthybius learned of the suspicious circumstances surrounding the death of the bard Pelagon.

After they had talked for a while of the degree to which King Nauplius of Euboea might be involved in conspiracies against Agamemnon, Neleus went on to warn Talthybius that it would be as well to warn his master that the son of Thyestes had also been seen travelling the Isthmus road.

'Aegisthus? You think he's up to something?'

'When was he ever not?'

'Does the Queen know of this?'

'Who knows what the Queen knows?' Neleus answered. 'She's always kept her own counsel. But her spies are all over Argos like lice on a mangy dog. If *I* know, then chances are that she does too.'

Talthybius withdrew into silence, pondering both what he had been told and the tone in which it was offered. As her loyal appointee – it was on the Queen's advice that Agamemnon had made him his chief herald many years earlier – he had secretly supplied Clytaemnestra with intelligence throughout the war; but the flow of information had been entirely one way. He had never received anything more than the occasional briefly worded demand in response. So he was now, he realised, entirely in the dark about recent developments in Mycenae, and the realisation left him more uneasy than he would have expected.

As soon as he arrived in the citadel late the following after-noon, Talthybius was admitted to Clytaemnestra's presence. This was the first time the herald had seen the Lion House for more than ten years and he was taken aback by the scale of the changes there. Though he was filled with admiration at the porphyry friezes and the gilded statuary and the stirring new frescoes with which the palace now commemorated some of the great deeds of the war, he could not help wondering how fully his master had been kept informed of the degree to which the hard-won booty of the Lydian campaign had been swallowed up by his wife's appetite for grandeur. He was more troubled, however, by the absence of familiar faces among the court officials, particularly in the busy secretariats that dealt with home security and foreign affairs. Admittedly he had been allowed only a brief glance around the humming chambers before he was conducted along the passages leading to the Queen's apartment. Nevertheless he was dismayed

to note that, if it had not been for the chamberlain's announce-
ment of his name, not one of those serious young men would
have known who he was.

Yet the Queen, when he came into her presence, welcomed
him as warmly as a long-missed friend. Though she was clearly
ruffled by his reports of the number of ships feared lost, she
contained her feelings, declaring that at least the war was over
and won at last, and nothing should be allowed to diminish the
scale of that triumph. Her questions showed a lively interest in
the part he had played in the more famous episodes of the war
– the embassies to Priam's court, the duel between Paris and
Menelaus, the dire problems posed by the quarrel between
Agamemnon and Achilles, the negotiations with the Trojan
defector Antenor. She listened with particular care to his account
of the fate of the Trojan women after the city had fallen, and if
she detected a certain delicate reserve when he came to speak
about Cassandra, she gave no sign of it.

Eventually Clytaemnestra declared that she was not unaware of
the streak of meanness in her husband and how it often left his
servants feeling undervalued. Talthybius need have no fear of such
treatment. The Queen would make certain that he was generously rewarded for all the loyal services he had rendered both to
the High King and, more discreetly, to herself. He could relax in
the knowledge that his future was assured.

More wine was served and the servant dismissed. Then the two
of them were alone together and therefore able – Clytaemnestra
insisted on it – to speak freely and in complete confidence.

'We are old friends, you and I,' she said, 'I know that I can
trust you.'

Talthybius warmed to her rueful smile. If the lines of her face
had grown more severe with the years, a rare intelligence was
evident everywhere in her grave eyes and the subtly understated
sensuality of her pursed lips. Not for the first time he felt his own
customary detachment yield to the brief touch of her hand.

'Agamemnon and I have seen each other only once in the past

ten years,' she said, 'and you will remember what happened on that occasion.' She took in the herald's uneasy nod and the movement in his throat. 'The truth is that my husband has become a stranger to me now. So tell me, Talthybius – you who have observed him more closely than anyone else for many years – is there anything further that I have to fear from him?'

Talthybius shifted in his seat. His eyes moved away from the disarming entreaty of her gaze to where the yellow blossoms dangling at her balcony glowed against the bruised blue of the evening sky. For the first time in all his years of double service he was unnervingly apprised of what it might mean to be caught in a narrow pass between the most powerful man in the western world and the most powerful woman.

It was not, for all the Queen's sympathetic assurances, the most comfortable place to be.

Clytaemnestra divined his difficulties. She smiled, soothed the back of his hand with the touch of her cool palm, and frankly admitted that after the atrocity at Aulis she could not pretend that there were any tender feelings left in her heart for Agamemnon. Her only interest was in the truth and, for that very reason, Talthybius should entertain no reservations about speaking his mind where her husband was concerned. She wanted to hear only the truth from his lips without any diplomatic hesitation about whether or not she would find it palatable.

A further silence ensued. 'I sense,' she said quietly, 'that you are keeping something from me. It will be better for us all if you share what you know.'

Talthybius released through a heavy sigh the tension in his chest.

'There is,' he said, 'the matter of Cassandra.'

At that moment Cassandra was standing alone in a chamber of the fort at Aulis in a state as close to complete mental derangement as she had experienced since the terrible moment, almost half her lifetime ago, of rejection by the god. Almost as soon as she set foot on firm ground in Argos she had felt her powers begin to return, cloudily at first, unresolved as a neuralgic ache that left her feeling giddy and light-headed; but then with greater force, like a sudden drop in atmospheric pressure presaging a storm. Then, on entering this private chamber, her heart had begun to beat more quickly, her breath came in quick, panting gasps, her whole body began to shake, and she knew that the oracular god had seized her.

When such fits had come upon her at home in Troy, her sisters and servants had always been at hand to care for her; but here, in this foreign land, she was alone apart from those women of Aulis who had been ordered to attend to her needs. To them she was no more than a captive daughter of the enemy – a haughty, distracted creature that, for reasons best known to himself, the High King had chosen as his concubine. They stared at her as though she was some exotic specimen from a zoo, remarking on the elaborate way she dressed her hair, and the muskiness of her perfume, with an impudence that failed to conceal their envy and contempt. And they had neither understanding nor sympathy for her plight when the prophetic spirit took possession of her.

To be surrounded by hostile, gawping strangers was a torment, but Cassandra held on just long enough to drive them from the room. As soon as they were gone, her consciousness dissolved into a stultifying sense of fear – not her own fear but the panic of a young girl whose shade was still inhabiting this chamber. Perhaps thirteen years old, she wore a saffron tunic with a coronet of flowers braided in her hair. The dappled skin of a fawn was tied about her shoulders. Her teeth were chattering. And her mind was seized by a terror so great that she could neither think nor speak. Until just a few moments ago this girl had believed that she had been brought here to prepare for her wedding; now she had learned that death was the only bridegroom she would meet that day. She was trying to remember exactly what she had been told; yet what had seemed to make sense when she was first told it had become incomprehensible to her now.

She was to be offered up as a sacrifice to an offended goddess. The man who had given that offence was her father, Agamemnon. It was he who would be waiting for her at the altar-stone. It would be he who wielded the knife.

Outside the chamber a mighty wind banged at the doors and windows. It gusted inside the girl's mind as she stared into the darkness that was waiting for her. She had been told that if she did not go consenting to the sacrifice then all her father's hopes would be wrecked and disaster must ensue. Yet she had always tried to be an obedient daughter. She had always tried to serve Divine Artemis with all her heart. So what had she done to deserve this fate? Why had the goddess turned her face against her? Terror was beating inside her like a bronze gong. Iphigenaia had never felt so utterly alone. Never had she been so afraid.

And that loneliness, that terror, overwhelmed Cassandra now. Even as she opened her eyes to find herself alone inside a silent chamber where no wind battered at the casement, the dread remained with her, helpless and hollow; intolerably, unappeasably her own. Her hands were shaking still. The commotion of her heart was the panic of a trapped bird.

If he was not yet in a state of mortal terror, Talthybius was fighting a rising tide of anxiety as he became increasingly aware of the isolation of his position.

With all the discretion he had acquired through a lifetime of court diplomacy, he had informed Clytaemnestra of her husband's incomprehensible passion for Cassandra. Watching the Queen's face harden as she listened, he had expected to become the hapless object of her rage; but it felt rather as if the temperature in the room had dropped. Clytaemnestra's eyes were as cold as her mind. When his account had faltered to its end, she merely nodded and said, 'And is this Trojan woman very beautiful?

Talthybius glanced up and noticed how the skin around the Queen's eyes and at the corners of her mouth had begun to pucker and wrinkle with age.

'There are those who would say so,' he prevaricated.

'Are you among them?'

'Cassandra is . . .' He hesitated. 'She has a certain strange allure.'

'And does Agamemnon mean to make her his queen?'

The herald's mouth was dry after the wine. 'The High King entrusts me with many things,' he said, 'but the secrets of his heart are not among them.'

Clytaemnestra nodded. 'You were ever a loyal servant.' However she did not smile. 'The question is, to whom are you more loyal – my husband or myself?'

'I would like to think,' he answered quietly, 'that there need be no conflict there.'

'Do not,' she said, 'be disingenuous with me.'

He was about to protest but she silenced him with a raised finger. 'Tell me,' she demanded, 'what instructions did Agamemnon give you when he sent you here?'

Alarmed by the sudden frostiness of her manner, Talthybius saw that he could afford to make no assumptions about this woman's good will.

'I was sent,' he said, 'to inform you of his wishes concerning the triumphal ceremony that would await him in Mycenae. After the loss of so many ships, he is anxious that there be no needless extravagance. He has asked me to supervise the arrangements – in close consultation with your majesty, of course.'

Brushing that aside, Clytaemnestra said, 'And did he not also ask you to prepare a report on his Queen and on her management of affairs in Mycenae?'

Talthybius tried for a weary little smile. 'The High King is too concerned by developments in Thessaly to waste time worrying over his confidence in you.'

'Do you know,' Clytaemnestra said quietly, placing the palms of her hands together and raising the tips of her fingers to her chin, 'I'm not sure that I entirely believe you, Talthybius?'

She saw his eyes shift away. She observed the tip of his tongue dampening his lips. He said, 'Have I not always served you well?'

'To the best of my knowledge you have,' she conceded, smiling. 'But then I'm quite sure that my husband must think the same of you; and I greatly fear, old friend, that the time has come for you to choose.'

As they advanced to the acclaim of the crowds from Aulis to Thebes and Megara, and then through town after town along the Isthmus road towards Mycenae, Agamemnon's composure swiftly returned. Yes, he might have lost half his fleet to Poseidon's rage, and half the treasure of Troy might have sunk to the bottom with it, but he remained the mightiest monarch that Argos had ever seen. His noble grandfather Pelops was a mere provincial by comparison. The kingdoms he had ruled in the west were only a portion of the domains that acknowledged the High King of Mycenae as their suzerain; and not even Theseus or Jason, adventurous spirits though they were, had crossed the ocean to destroy a kingdom as wealthy and powerful as Troy.

And all these people gathered in the streets, strewing the path of his chariot with flowers and singing hymns of praise, or running down from their hillside farms and holding up their children to see him as he passed – all of them adored and feared him as the King of Men. Also the weather had cleared at last. Bright winter sunshine glittered off the harness of his team, dazzling the eyes of those who stared up at him in wonder. Had it not been for a baleful stomach, Agamemnon might almost have been in awe of his own magnificence.

Lines of armed infantrymen marched at either side of the procession, keeping the more importunate spectators at bay and guarding the ox-drawn wagons that carried Agamemnon's immense share of the plunder. Ahead of them, and far enough behind the High King's chariot not to be troubled by the dust rising from its wheels, Cassandra rode inside a litter that was carried on poles by slaves. Gauzy veils hung from its roof so that she could look out from where she reclined on cushions and see the Argive peasantry squinting at the litter through the sun's cold glare, but they could make out no more than a vague shadow of her form. She was remembering the day, many years earlier, when Paris had entered Troy in triumph with Helen carried behind him in much the same way. How strange the world was with its reversals of fortune! How comprehensive the imagination of the gods that all those reversals had been foreseen!

She had herself experienced such a strange, transfiguring reversal not long ago in that haunted chamber in Aulis. It had happened only moments after she had been inhabited by the shade of Iphigenaia, and the terror was still with her. She had been lying on the couch with her teeth chattering and her arms clutched across her breast, holding her shoulders for protection against the world, when she sensed a sudden change around her. Everything was silent, yet it was as though a deep-searching chord of music had been struck from a lyre. Now the air of the chamber was calm and filled with expectation. In an atmosphere so serene that it was impossible to sustain the fear, Cassandra understood that Iphigenaia had been standing in the presence of a god. Artemis, protector of virgins, on whose altar she was shortly to be sacrificed, had come to take the girl up in her kindly embrace. Even before Agamemnon offered his daughter up to the goddess, the goddess had already come to claim her. Iphigenaia had known herself under her protection. There could be, after all, nothing to fear.

Yet when Cassandra opened her eyes it was not the serene face of Artemis that smiled down at her, but the benevolent, far-sighted gaze of Divine Apollo, who was twin brother to the goddess. And she too knew in those moments that the god had no more abandoned her all those years ago in Thymbra than his sister, Divine Artemis, had ever turned her face away from Iphigenaia. He had always watched over her. He would be there, at her side, throughout the ordeal to come.

And with that knowledge the confusions that had darkened Cassandra's mind for more than half her young lifetime came through at last into clear solution.

How was it that she could ever have come to believe that she had been rejected by the god?

It was because, she remembered now, the high priest of Apollo at Thymbra had told everyone that Apollo had rejected her. The priest was an old man whom she had always held in awe and veneration. His name was Aesacus and it was to him that she turned for guidance when Far-sighted Apollo had visited her in a dream, asking her to become his sibyl. She had told her father of the dream and her father had sent her to Aesacus. The priest and the girl had spent many hours together while he instructed her in the mysteries of Apollo. And then, one hot afternoon – and it was this memory that had been distorted and erased by the shock of subsequent events – the old man had laid hands on her. They were alone together that day. She had been reclining with her eyes closed and her body entirely relaxed in the discipline of meditation when he loomed over her and put his hand to her breast. Shocked and dismayed by the expression on his face, she had tried to shrug his hand away. But he was stronger than she was. His weight moved over her body. She could feel him groping between her legs, tugging the skirt of her dress up around her thighs. He was making little shushing sounds as he murmured that the true service of the god required that she deliver herself over to him body and soul. She must understand, he said, that her body was no longer her own to command. As the servant of Apollo, Cassandra must do everything that the god required of her.

The thirteen-year-old girl had lain stiff as an effigy beneath the old priest. But the noises he made and the warm stink of his breath frightened and disgusted her. She could see the idol of Apollo staring into the still air of the temple. Then it was hidden as the priest lowered his face towards her. She saw the damp curl of his tongue. Her arms were trapped beneath his weight. Having no other means to protect herself, she spat into his open mouth.

When Aesacus recoiled in disgust, his body shifted just enough for her to slip out from under it. Cassandra ran out of the temple into the clean, dry air.

Later, when he was summoned to speak before her father, Aesacus would be grave and mournful. As King Priam could surely tell from her confused attempts to libel his own good name, he said, it must be clear that Cassandra was far too unstable to serve as priestess to Apollo. He regretted to have to report it, but in her incontinent desire to be made High Priestess to the god, the girl had desecrated his temple by offering her body as a bribe. When Aesacus rebuffed her, she had poured her execrations on him. But the god would not be mocked, nor would he see his priest abused. Cassandra's words could not be believed, Aesacus declared, because Apollo had spat into her mouth so that all the prophecies she uttered would prove false.

Confronted on the one hand by an austere old man of the highest reputation and on the other by a hysterical daughter, King Priam had made his judgement. Eventually, with no one to believe her, Cassandra began to doubt the truth of her own experience. All she knew for sure was that the world placed no trust in the visions that came to her. But in those redemptive moments in Aulis, the shade of a girl who had also been betrayed by a father, had visited her like a messenger from the gods. Having shared all the desolations of fear together, they had seen that fear must pass. And now, as she lay alone in the swaying litter making its slow way to Mycenae, Cassandra drew strength from the certain knowledge that the gods always remained true to those who served them well.

They passed the last night of their journey only a few miles from the city in the hall of an old baron whose son had been killed in the war. The man's grief darkened the triumphal air of their arrival. The women began to wail. Depressed by the misery around him, Agamemnon retired early from the feast. Too weary and morose to make demands on Cassandra, he fell asleep, grumbling that these people had no understanding of what had been endured at Troy.

Sure now that this would be the last night they would pass on the face of the earth, Cassandra looked down where the recumbent figure of Agamemnon, King of Men, Sacker of Troy, lay snoring at her side. And if her heart was heavy, it was not only with an uneasy mingling of pity and contempt, but with an overwhelming sense of the pathos of all human circumstance.

Death in the Lion House

They entered Mycenae late the following afternoon. On their approach to the city, Agamemnon had proudly instructed Cassandra to peer out through the veils of her litter. She looked up and saw the grim bastions crouched on their crag. She heard the shouting of the crowd long before they passed under the gaze of the stone lions guarding the gateway to the citadel. She saw the light gleaming off the bronze plates of the high double doors and, though those doors remained wide open to admit the rest of Agamemnon's train, she felt as helplessly trapped inside the city as if the huge masonry blocks of which the walls were built had collapsed behind her. Sharp sunlight glinted everywhere, cold as the light off a winter stream, yet after the airy elegance of Troy, Mycenae shadowed her mind. Her heart quailed when her eyes fell on the ancestral graves inside those walls. She caught, like the hot stench rising off an abattoir, her first close sense of the obscene history of this city.

At the top of the steps beneath the entrance to the palace, Clytaemnestra stood waiting to greet her husband. Talthybius stood at her right, holding his herald's staff; on her left, Idas and Doricleus, counsellors who had both served Atreus well in the old days and had known Agamemnon since he was a boy, smiled to receive the returning king. But, as yet, Agamemnon had not allowed his eyes to alight on his wife. Even as he acknowledged the acclaim of the crowd on his approach to the palace, his eyes were taking in the prodigious scale of her expenditure on the city. Yes, Clytaemnestra had certainly made Mycenae a capital fit for a homecoming king of kings, but he was wondering how much of the wealth shipped back from the sacked cities of Asia could be left in his treasury after the bills had been met for the huge number of architects, quarry-masters, masons, sculptors and artists it must have taken to create this magnificence, let alone for all the materials, many of them precious and rare, used in the building? Also, despite his specific instructions to Talthybius that there should be no extravagant arrangements made for his return, richly woven cloths of purple and scarlet had been draped along the streets all the way from the Lion Gate to the palace steps. The hooves of his chariot team had trampled on them.

As his driver reined in the horses, Agamemnon glanced quickly across the crowd of ministers and officials who were cheering and applauding him where they stood behind the Queen. Gorgeously robed, they crowded the steps and portico, loudly proclaiming their allegiance. Yet he was surprised how few of those faces he immediately recognized.

Agamemnon reminded himself that he had been away from the city for ten years; everyone he knew must have changed in that time, and old retainers who had perished from disease and accidents would have been replaced. In any case, his true friends were behind him now, the veterans of the long war, those who had paid in wounds and endurance for the luxurious lives of these young stay-at-homes. Well, they would have their reward. He would see they profited from the changes he made now that he was back in control of the city's affairs. In the meantime, to a tumultuous roar, he raised his right hand in acknowledgement of his people's adulation. The Lion of Mycenae had come home.

From where she still cowered behind the veils of her litter some distance behind the High King's chariot, Cassandra heard the roar go up. Drums were beating. When she peered through a chink in the veils she saw a flock of startled doves rise from the roof of the palace in a clatter of wings. Then her eyes settled on the lean figure of the queen where she stood with her strong chin tilted, smiling up at Agamemnon in his chariot. She was smaller than Cassandra had expected, yet nevertheless imperious in her long, flounced gown, with gold flashing from her necklaces and bangles, its lustre brightened by contrast with the dark sheen of her hair.

And then, as if drawn by the intensity of Cassandra's gaze, Clytaemnestra turned her eyes on the litter as the carriers lowered it to the ground.

Reflexively Cassandra pulled back into the shade.

What was she to do? To draw the curtains and step out into the sunlight would be to attract the ferocity of that queenly stare. She could not bring herself to move. The shouts of the crowd became a roaring in her head. She huddled inside the veiled litter and watched a delirium of pictures forming in her mind. The scarlet cloths covering the steps to the Lion House turned to a torrent of blood. Someone had put out the sun. Mycenae became a city of ghosts and night. Cassandra's mind was in flight, moving swiftly along dark corridors. Murder and malice, hatred and vengeance polluted this city's sky. The air was thick and toxic. This palace was a butcher's cave, the streets runnels of blood. From generation to generation no one was safe. In Mycenae only the dead survived.

Cassandra recoiled back against the cushions, squinting against a sudden crash of light. Then a suave voice was saying, 'Come, lady, your presence will shortly be required.' When she opened her eyes she was looking into the tense face of Talthybius who was offering his hand.

Calling on Apollo to defend her and the Earth Mother to support her, Cassandra stepped into her fate.

He had postponed the moment for as long as he could – making dispositions for his retinue, receiving the greetings and congratulations of old friends, quietly ordering Talthybius to look to

Cassandra's welfare, then making a long and solemn show of his ritual offering of thanks to the gods; but now they were alone together in the private apartment of the palace. Recalling how the last time he had seen his wife she had been transformed into a demented Fury by her hatred for what he was about to do, Agamemnon was still uncertain what to say to her. He knew she was watching him now as he took off his helmet and began to undo the buckles of his leathers. It seemed she had no intention of making this easy for him. There had always been a severe edge to Clytaemnestra's high-boned features and the years had done nothing to soften it. He found it hard even to look at her directly now.

Agamemnon heaved a weary sigh. For centuries to come the bards would remember him as the conqueror of Troy, but in this private apartment of the Lion House he would forever remain the monster who had sacrificed his daughter. And that terrible business at Aulis might have won him a fair wind back to the war but it had left deep lesions on his mind; and it made everything impossible back here in Argos. Above all, as far as he and his wife were concerned, it had abolished any possibility of truth.

Taking in the unfamiliar, sweetish odour of the incense burning in this chamber, he said, 'I see you've spared no expense on improving the city.'

If there was criticism in his tone, she chose to ignore it.

'I thought,' she said, 'that Mycenae should properly reflect your glory.'

'It feels more like your city than mine,' he muttered a little peevishly. 'I shall have to do something about that.'

'You are the King.'

'Yes,' he answered, fumbling with a stiff buckle at his hip, 'I am the King.'

A vault of silence closed down round them, from which, it seemed for a time, there might be no escape. Then she surprised him by sighing as a wife will who despairs of her husband's ham-fistedness.

'Here,' she took a step towards him. 'Let me help you with that.'

He hesitated for a moment, wondering whether he would prefer to call for his body-servant; then he relaxed his shoulders and turned into her reach. A moment later she was lifting the heavy corselet from his back.

Sighing again, he sat down, reached for the wine that had been poured and took a swig. 'It feels as though I've been locked in armour for the last ten years.'

'Then it will be good to put it down. The slaves are heating water for you in the bath-house. You have done well,' she conceded. 'It's time to take your ease.'

But he did not entirely trust this muted benevolence.

'Not for long,' he said. 'Not if there's any substance in the reports I've been getting from the north.'

'The Myrmidons are holding the Dorian advance,' she quietly replied. 'The son of Achilles will not let them pass.'

'You are confident of that?'

'The Dorians invaded only because they thought the Lion of Mycenae had his hands full at Troy. But Troy is finished. After the destruction you've made, your name is feared everywhere. Now that you are home they will withdraw.'

'I hope you're right.' He glanced across at her, reluctant to reveal the anxiety behind his question. 'Have you heard about these new weapons they wield?'

'Agents have already been placed behind their lines. Sooner or later they will find out the secret. Then we too shall have such weapons.'

Impressed by the quiet authority of her tone, he studied his wife with an involuntary surge of the admiration that this formidable woman always inspired in him. Surely other men must feel it too. So had she taken a lover from among them while he was away? The reports from Pelagon had always assured him of her fidelity; but Pelagon had died and Agamemnon had heard nothing since. And ten years was a damnably long time for any woman to nurse her virtue. He would make discreet enquiries of Idas and Doricleus. If there was cause for concern they would have caught wind of it.

But he glanced away wondering whether such suspicious thoughts demeaned him. Could the earth have a stronger or more resourceful queen to show than this one had proved herself to be? Agamemnon very much doubted it. And in any case Clytaemnestra was Queen here only because he was King, and it was evident that she enjoyed that queenly power too much to surrender it lightly. With a little cunning it ought to be possible, therefore, to retain her invaluable services while looking to Cassandra to supply his more intimate needs. Like harnessing a new pair of horses to the chariot, he thought, it was all a question of handling.

'If I was able to give all my thought to winning the war at Troy,' he began, 'it was only because I could rest in the knowledge that Mycenae was in safe hands.'

Clytaemnestra nodded her acknowledgement. The nuances of movement about her lips might almost have suggested a smile.

Agamemnon also nodded. 'There'll be time enough for you to give me a full report tomorrow. But you too have done well. Come and sit down with me.' He sighed as she chose a seat by the window some distance across the floor from him. Something further was required. With a loose hand he gestured towards the frescoes on the chamber walls. 'I even approve of some of these changes you've made.' Though in truth he did not at all care for the painting on which his eyes fell at that moment. As far as he could make out, it showed the occasion on which Zeus had been bound with rawhide thongs by his wife Hera and the other Olympian gods. It would be wiser, however, not to reveal his distaste for it. Not yet at least.

Then another thought occurred to him. 'Where are the children? Why is Orestes not here to witness his father's triumph?' Only after the words were out did he recognize how close they brought him to perilous ground. Was she hiding her children from him out of some irrational fear that he might do them harm?

But she answered him calmly enough. 'They are with King Strophius in Phocis. Orestes is greatly attached to the king's son Pylades. He is safe enough there.'

'He would be safer still with me here in Mycenae.'

'I know.' Clytaemnestra glanced away, and back again. 'And he is disappointed to miss your triumph. But I had reason to leave him in Phocis for the time being.' She did not flinch from the interrogative glare in his narrowed eyes. 'Consider this,' she said, '– it is all of ten years since you and I were alone in each other's company. The truth is we are little more than strangers to each other now. I felt that we needed time to renew our life together. Time to try to heal the harm that has been done. There will be time enough for the children when that is accomplished.' She drew in her breath. He saw the effort that this declaration had required. He respected her truth when she added, 'It will not be easily done.'

Almost grateful that she had decided to breach the silence between them before it became impassable, he said, a little hoarsely, 'I do not forget the grief I have given you.'

Where she sat in her chair by the window, Clytaemnestra closed her eyes like a woman in pain. She shook her head, not evidently in refusal of his appeasing gesture, but as an indication of the gravity of that pain. With the long fingers of her left hand she stroked her cheek.

'I even concede,' he said, 'that I may have given you cause to hate me.'

He had left an opportunity for her to offer some answering word of demurral. When no word came he flushed and looked away. Already he was regretting this rash impulse of conciliation. But having said so much he must say more.

'We were all in the hands of the gods.' He tapped his clenched fist against the arm of his chair. 'I had no desire to do what I did . . . How could any man? But you must understand that I was left with no choice. I had no choice at all.'

Clytaemnestra gazed out of the window at where the sky had reddened above the mountains, casting a hectic glow on the high slopes of snow. Soon those clouds would be ferrying dusk across the plain. Sounds of revelry rose from the streets below. The air was savoury with the smell of an ox roasting on a spit.

'Yes,' she quietly averred, 'sometimes the gods leave us with no choice.'

A silence settled between them. He took a measure of satisfaction in it. Were there to be no recriminations then? Had the passage of time taught her some philosophy; or was her pragmatic spirit sufficiently appeased by the fact of his victory and the wealth that came with it?

'And look,' he risked after a time, 'evil it may have been, but see what good has come of it. Haven't we done what we set out to do? The treasure of Troy is ours.'

'Yes,' she concurred, 'we have done what we set out to do.'

'And the past is the past. We cannot change it; but need it haunt us for ever?'

He looked across at her with the mild urgency of a man appealing to reason. 'Can we not put a stop to it?'

As though impelled by a residual impulse of affection, she smiled at him wanly.

'Yes,' she whispered to the evening air, 'I believe we can put a stop to it.'

'Good,' he said simply, pouring himself more wine. And again, 'Good.'

He took a drink and felt his head swim a little. This wine was strongly mixed. When he looked up from the goblet he saw that she was watching as he wiped the back of his hand across his beard. Evidently she had not yet finished with him. Some other issue was pressing on her mind. Then it occurred to him that if she had spies in place behind the Dorian lines, then she might also have kept spies behind his own. Did she already know something about Cassandra? If so, it might be better to have it out now while this air of truce prevailed.

'Well?' he demanded.

'I was wondering,' she said, 'do you have news of my sister?'

Relieved to find himself on easier ground, Agamemnon sniffed and grunted. 'Not a word. Not since she and my brother sailed from Troy.'

'You decided to let her live then?'

'It was his choice. If it had been left to me . . .' Agamemnon stared into his wine, shaking his head. 'I don't understand the man . . . To take her back like that, after all the humiliation and pain she's caused him.'

He looked up and caught a wry, ironic glint in Clytaemnestra's eyes.

'Perhaps Menelaus has also decided that the past is the past,' she said.

For a moment he thought she might be mocking him.

But she got to her feet and said. 'You must be weary. Come, your bath is prepared. Let me help to soothe your limbs.' She took the golden combs from her hair so that the piled coiffure fell in a black cascade about her shoulders. Then she held out her hands to raise him from his chair. 'The war is won. You have shown yourself for what you truly are. The world knows it and all your troubles will soon be at an end. From today,' she smiled, 'everything will be different. I promise you.'

Astonished and mollified by the alteration in her manner, he got up and followed her through to the bath-house where steam was rising from the sunken bath that had been heated for him. Nereids and dolphins danced together against the azure blue of the walls. The humid air was fragrant with perfumes and scented oils. His own body-servant stood waiting there along with three women from the palace, but Clytaemnestra dismissed them all. 'The King desires to be alone with his Queen,' she declared. 'I will attend to his needs myself.'

As the servants left by the door leading to their quarters, Agamemnon pursed his lips in a smile of gratified surprise. He had not fucked this woman for more than ten years and in all that time she had lacked the consolations that had been available to him. This lioness must be on heat. And once she was replete and satisfied, he thought, it might be much easier to raise the matter of Cassandra.

He moved to take her into his embrace but Clytaemnestra placed the palm of her hand at his chest and pushed him, smiling, towards the bench of white marble that stood beside the pool. 'First,' she said, 'you must take your bath.'

Already erect, he opened his hands in appeal.

'Go,' she reprimanded him lightly. 'Disrobe.'

Like an obedient boy, he turned to do as he was bidden, shuffling off his sandals and pulling his dark red linen robe over his head and shoulders. Admiring the lines of her figure where she bent over to gather towels from a chest, he slipped out of his kilt and drawers and stood naked in the steam from the bath, suddenly conscious of the aches and pains locked into his limbs. He flexed the sinews of his arms and pushed his hands back through the mane of his loosened hair. Though he had put on weight since Clytaemnestra had last seen him this way, he was still, he thought, a handsome figure of a man; and if his skin was etched like a butcher's block with the many wounds he had taken, they were all honourable scars, the signature of his valour and virility.

'Look,' he said, displaying his body, arms outstretched, as she came towards the massage table with a bundle of soft towels in her arms, 'here is a map of the war at Troy. I have good tales to tell about each of these scars.' With the tip of a stubby finger he traced the white ridge that ran along his upper right arm, almost from the elbow to the shoulder. 'This is the gash I got from a Trojan spear on the day they drove us back to the ships. The host panicked when they saw me bleeding. Odysseus and Diomedes also took wounds that day, and Achilles was out of the fight, sulking in his lodge. For a time I thought it was all up with us.'

But she had, it seemed, discouragingly little interest in his story. 'Get into the bath,' she urged. 'You can brag of your valour to me while you soak.'

In mock offence he pouted his lips at her. She answered with a haughty toss of her head and laid the heaped towels carefully on the table. Turning away from her, Agamemnon walked across the tiles towards the bath. He was about to step down into its soothing heat when he was struck by another thought. He looked back to share it just in time to see her standing as a fisherman stands at the prow of his boat when he casts a net. Then something swooped in a widening loop towards him. It came at him through the air like a silent cloud of bees, and before he had time to understand what was happening, the meshes fell in a gauzy shower over his head and shoulders, and then dropped down across his arms and thighs. Perplexed and shocked, he was raising his arms to push the coarse grey blur away from his body when she tugged with both hands on the slender length of rope she held and the net tightened around his limbs.

He was shouting now. Still able to keep his balance on his bare feet, but tangled like a maddened bear inside the trammels of the net and scarcely able to move his arms and legs, Agamemnon twisted his body round to confront his wife. He saw Clytaemnestra walking towards him with a sword gripped in both hands. Its pommel trembled close to her chin; the blade angled down in front of her breasts; but his eyes were fixed on the pallid mask of hatred that was her face.

In the moment when Agamemnon saw that his wife was about to murder him, she raised her arms above her head and brought the blade down with all her might, through the toils of the net, into the broad target of his chest where he felt the breast-bone shatter.

He might have fallen then from the force of the thrust, but his ribs were caught on the blade and the pressure of her grip on the hilt supported him. For a few seconds they stood together, face to face, conjoined by the sword, staring into each other's eyes as the steam rose round them. Both were sweating in the moist air, though neither was now entirely in this world.

Agamemnon coughed, choking on something deep in his throat

that should not be there. Harm had been done to his breathing. The channels of his ears were loud with noise. Each part of his body had begun to panic like a routed army. He knew that he could no longer count on the strength of his legs.

Leaning forward, with a twist of her wrists Clytaemnestra tugged the sword free; and felt the frisky spatter of blood across her face.

He staggered as his head went down. Now he was spluttering on the froth of blood and spittle bubbling in his mouth. Agamemnon raised his chin and saw, through the mesh of the net, an unsightly red smear staining her cheek as she wiped the back of her wrist across her eyes. Was she wounded too? Was the blood his or hers? No matter, for he was trying to spit his throat clear of obstructions so that he could breathe again when the sword came back at him.

The blade swung in lower this time, held in only one hand, yet entering his naked belly with alarming ease. The force of it winded him. Sodden air gushed upwards from his punctured lung. As the sword slid out again terrible things had already begun to happen in places he couldn't see. Nor could he even raise his arms to hug himself. A huge tidal wave of self-pity pushed Agamemnon down to his knees. Blood had splashed on the tiles. He knelt in a gathering pool of it, gasping and wheezing there. This was no way for the King of Men to die. There was neither justice nor glory in it. He refused to die like this.

Summoning his failing reserves of strength, Agamemnon lifted his head; but his eyes were bleary with tears when he looked up again.

He saw the figure of a woman standing near him and, in a quick flurry of relief, thought that he recognized Cassandra. Yes, she would come to help him now when help was needed. She would comfort and succour him. She would wipe this mess from his mouth and take him to her breasts where her nipples stood dark and sweet as figs. He tried to hold out his hand to her but the toils of the net prevented him. In a sputtering of blood he whispered her name.

'Have patience,' the woman hissed, 'your Trojan whore will lie beside you soon enough.' And he heard the hatred there and saw that he was mistaken, for the face that stared at him was the face of Clytaemnestra after all.

And there are two figures standing before him now, neither of them clear, neither of them quite stable. They are looking not at him but at each other and both their mouths are agape. They might be shouting, both at the same time, but he cannot be sure because of the hollow roar gusting through his ears. One of them is his wife wearing a blood-stained gown; but the other? A man, yes, but who among his subjects could stand and look on and do nothing while this dreadful harm was done to him?

Before Agamemnon can make out the features of that face, his own head droops on his neck and he is vomiting blood and bile and the wine he has drunk. His beard stinks of his dying. He wants to lie down. That's all he wants, and it's little enough to ask when he is in such pain, but someone has crouched down in front of him and is holding up his chin in the tight pluck of a finger and thumb. Through the trammels of the net a man's face sneers into his own. As if against a strong gale, a voice is asking, 'Do you know me, cousin?'

Agamemnon knows only that time and breath and light are running out on him.

When he shakes his head he is merely trying to clear the thick, obstructing slobber from his throat, but the man takes it for an answer.

'I am Aegisthus,' he hisses, 'son of Thyestes. Now do you know me?' He holds up the bronze blade before Agamemnon's bewildered eyes. 'This is the sword with which my mother killed herself. This is the sword with which I took righteous vengeance for my father by slaying yours. And this, dear brother in treachery, is the sword with which I mean to cleanse the world of you.'

But Agamemnon is no longer present to feel the blade intruding on his flesh. He has been watching Troy burn again; he has seen Menelaus and Odysseus, Ajax and Diomedes laughing at his side, and his mighty fleet of ships flexing their oars against the glitter of the sea; and here now is his father, King Atreus, grim-faced and resolute as he watches his wife drowning in the Bay of Argos. And then, only a moment or two later, after a little, clumsy fall over which he has no control at all, Agamemnon is down there in the water with his mother, feeling the warmth beneath the surface, letting it enter him, becoming it, as Poseidon grips him by the hair and tugs him down into green shadows and the last light spins away.

Anxiety on Ithaca

Of almost all the events I have related in this scroll we Ithacans remained in ignorance for some considerable time. Though we are not so remote from the citadels of power across the mainland as are our reclusive northern neighbours, the Phaeacians of Scheria, our cluster of islands lies on the western fringes of the great world, away from the major channels of communication. For that reason, it is perhaps unsurprising that Troy should have fallen, or that the Lion of Mycenae should have met his death in his own bath-house at the hands of his wife, without our hearing of these events until news of them was already old elsewhere.

Nevertheless, it was one of our own island people whose skill and intelligence had largely determined the course of the war, and what is more surprising is the fact that, even as we Ithacans lived in ignorance of his fate, so too did all the other kingdoms of Argos. For those among us who had been close to Lord Odysseus before he sailed for Troy, that ignorance became a cause for increasing anxiety, and it now remains to tell what happened among us on Ithaca at that time, and to report the truth of what we eventually learned of the adventures which shaped the destiny of Odysseus after the fall of Troy. That truth is, I believe, still stranger and more powerful than the many fables later attached to his name.

Glossary of Characters

Deities

Aphrodite	Goddess of many aspects, mostly associated with Love and Beauty
Apollo	God with many aspects, including Prophecy, Healing, Pestilence and the Arts
Ares	God of War, twin brother of Eris
Artemis	Virgin Goddess of the Wild
Athena	Goddess with many aspects, including Wisdom, Power and Protection
Boreas	God of the North Wind
Dionysus	God of wine
Eris	Goddess of Strife and Discord, twin sister to Ares
Eros	God of Love, son of Aphrodite
Hephaestus	God of fire and craftsmanship
Hera	Goddess Queen of Olympus, wife of Zeus, presides over marriage
Hermes	God with many aspects, including eloquence, imagination, invention. A slippery fellow
Neith	Libyan Goddess of Lake Tritonis
Persephone	Goddess of the Underworld, wife of Hades and daughter of Demeter

Poseidon	God with many aspects, ruler of the Sea, Earthquakes and Horses
Zeus	King of Olympus, ruler of the gods

Mortals

Acamas	Argive warrior, son of Theseus
Acastus	King of Iolcus
Achilles	son of Peleus and Thetis, leader of the Myrmidons, father of Neoptolemus
Aeacus	King of Aegina, father of Peleus and Telamon
Aegisthus	son of Thyestes, cousin to Agamemnon and Menelaus
Aeneas	Prince of the Dardanians
Aeolus	King of Aeolia, father of Canace and Macareus
Aesacus	priest of Apollo at Thymbra
Aethra	mother of Theseus, once Queen of Troizen, now bondswoman to Helen
Agamemnon	son of Atreus, King of Mycenae, High King of Argos
Agialeia	Lady of Tiryns, wife of Diomedes
Aias	Locrian captain
Ajax	Argive hero, son of Telamon, cousin of Achilles
Alcinous	King of Scheria, father of Nausicaa
Amphinomus	prince of Dulichion, son of Nisus, friend and suitor to Penelope
Andromache	wife of Hector
Antenor	counsellor to Priam
Anticleia	mother of Odysseus, wife of King Laertes
Antilochus	son of Nestor
Antinous	son of Eupeithes, suitor to Penelope
Aerope	Queen of Mycenae, wife of Atreus and mother of Agamemnon and Menelaus
Arete	wife of King Alcinous and mother of Nausicaa
Astyanax	son of Hector and Andromache

Atreus	King of Mycenae, brother of Thyestes and father of Agamemnon and Menelaus
Axylus	a Zacynthian sailor
Baius	helmsman on *The Fair Return*
Briseis	Dardanian maiden captured by Achilles
Calchas	Trojan priest of Apollo who defects to the Argives
Calypso	priestess of Aiaia, sibyl at Cuma, and lover of Odysseus
Canace	daughter of King Aeolus and sister of Macareus
Capys	son of King Priam
Cassandra	daughter of King Priam
Cheiron	King of the Centaurs
Chryseis	daughter of Apollo's priest in Thebe, captive of Agamemnon
Cinyras	King of Cyprus
Circe	High Priestess of Aiaia
Clitus	sailor on *The Fair Return*
Clymene	Andromache's serving woman
Clytaemnestra	Queen of Mycenae, daughter of Tyndareus & Leda, wife of Agamemnon.
Ctesippus	son of Polytherses, suitor to Penelope
Deidameia	daughter of King Lycomedes, mother of Neoptolemus by Achilles
Deiphobus	son of King Priam
Demodocus	bard of Scheria
Demonax	captain of *The Swordfish*
Demophon	brother of Acamas. Son of Theseus
Diomedes	Lord of Tiryns, Argive hero
Diotima	wise woman on Ithaca
Dolon	fisherman of Ithaca
Doricleus	counsellor at Mycenae

Electra	daughter of Agamemnon & Clytaemnestra
Elpenor	Ithacan warrior and sailor on *The Fair Return*
Eteoneus	chief minister of Sparta
Eumaeus	farmer and herdsman of Ithaca
Eupeithes	a nobleman of Ithaca and father of Antinous
Eurybates	Herald of Ithaca
Eurycleia	servant of Anticleia, formerly nurse to Odysseus
Eurylochus	lieutenant to Odysseus
Eurymachus	suitor to Penelope
Eurynomus	son of Aegyptius, suitor to Penelope
Glaucus	captain of the *Nereid*
Grinus	Ithacan warrior and sailor on *The Fair Return*
Guneus	Thessalian warrior and captain
Halitherses	soothsayer of Ithaca
Hanno	nomad of the Garamantes
Hattusilis	Emperor of the Hittites
Hector	eldest son of King Priam
Hecuba	Queen of Troy, wife of Priam and mother of Hector
Helen	daughter of Tyndareus/Zeus and Leda. Queen of Sparta, wife of Menelaus.
Heracles	hero
Hermes	Libyan boy
Hermione	daughter of Menelaus and Helen
Hylax	Phoenician trader
Icarius	Spartan nobleman, brother of Tyndareus, father of Penelope
Idas	Counsellor in Mycenae
Idomeneus	King of Crete
Iliona	Queen of Thracian Chersonese, wife of Polymnestor and daughter of Priam
Ilus	Grandfather of King Priam

Iphigenaia	daughter of Agamemnon & Clytaemnestra
Irus	Ithacan beggar
Jason	hero, leader of the Argonauts
Laertes	King of Ithaca, father of Odysseus
Laodice	daughter of King Priam
Laomedon	King of Troy, father of Priam
Leodes	priest of Apollo in Ithaca, suitor to Penelope
Macareus	son of King Aeolus and brother of Canace
Marpessa	serving woman to Clytaemnestra
Mastor	Ithacan warrior and sailor on *The Fair Return*
Meda	Queen of Crete and wife of Idomeneus
Medon	Ithacan herald
Meges	leader of the Dulichians
Melantho	serving woman to Penelope
Memnon	Trojan ally, leader of the Ethiopians
Menelaus	King of Sparta, husband of Helen, brother to Agamemnon
Menestheus	Argive captain, King of Athens
Mentes	Taphian ambassador
Mentor	nobleman of Ithaca
Molossus	son of Neoptolemus by Andromache
Mopsa	woman of Aiaia
Nauplius	King of Euboea, father of Palamedes
Nausicaa	daughter of King Alcinous
Neoptolemus	son of Achilles, also known as Pyrrhos
Nereids	fifty daughters of the sea-god Nereus
Nestor	King of Pylos
Nisus	King of Dulichion and father of Amphimonus
Odysseus	Lord of Ithaca
Orestes	son of Agamemnon and Clytaemnestra

Palamedes	Prince of Euboea, son of King Nauplius
Paris	son of King Priam, lover of Helen
Patroclus	son of Menoetius, beloved friend of Achilles
Peiraeus	friend of Phemius and Telemachus
Peisenor	herald of Ithaca
Peisistratus	son of Nestor
Pelagon	bard of Mycenae
Peleus	son of King Aeacus, father of Achilles
Pellas	Samian suitor to Penelope
Pelopia	daughter of Thyestes and second wife of Atreus, mother of Aegisthus
Pelops	father of Atreus and Thyestes, grandfather of Agamemnon
Penelope	daughter of Icarius, cousin to Helen and Clytaemnestra and wife of Odysseus
Perimedes	sailor on *The Fair Return*
Phemius	bard of Ithaca
Philoctetes	Aeolian archer
Philoetius	herdsman of Ithaca
Philona	friend of Nausicaa
Phoenix	Myrmidon warrior
Polites	Ithacan Lieutenant and sailor on *The Fair Return*
Polydamna	wise woman to Helen
Polydorus	youngest son of King Priam
Polymnestor	King of Thracian Chersonese
Polytherses	Lord of Same and father of Ctesippus
Polyxena	daughter of King Priam
Priam	son of Laomedon, King of Troy, also known as Podarces
Pylades	son of King Strophius and friend of Orestes
Sinon	cousin to Odysseus
Sthenelus	King of Mycenae
Strophius	King of Phocis and father of Pylades

Talthybius	Argive herald
Teiresias	Prophet at the Oracle of the Dead at Cuma
Telamon	father of Ajax and brother to Peleus
Telegonus	son of Odysseus and Circe
Telemachus	son of Odysseus and Penelope
Terpis	father of Phemius the Ithacan bard
Theano	high priestess of Athena in Troy, wife of Antenor
Theoclymenus	seer from Hyperesia
Thersites	Argive soldier and kinsman of Diomedes
Theseus	hero, King of Athens, conqueror of Crete
Thesprotus	King of Sicyon
Thetis	daughter of Cheiron, wife of Peleus and mother of Achilles
Thrasymedes	son of Nestor
Thyestes	brother of Atreus, uncle to Agamemnon and Menelaus, father of Aegisthus
Tyndareus	King of Sparta, father of Clytaemnestra and Helen, husband of Leda

Acknowledgements

Because the truth of myth is subtler than the truth of fact, myths never take a fixed and final form. Even among the early poets and tragedians of Greece, there were many variations, both of detail and substance, in the way those powerful tales were told. So any reworking of such mythic material must either choose among the available alternatives or tell it differently again. For that reason, and because I wanted to tell this story in a new way for our own time, readers already familiar with Homer's *Odyssey,* with the *Oresteia* of Aeschylus, and with the Trojan plays of Euripides, may have found that aspects of this novel ran counter to their expectations. Nevertheless my debt to those poets is immense, as also to Book VI of Vergil's *Aeneid,* to Ovid's account of Macareus in his *Metamorphoses,* and to Herodotus' description of the various tribes of Libya in Book IV of his *Histories.* If this novel encourages readers to return to those incomparable sources, or to visit them for the first time, then perhaps the unscholarly liberties I have taken with them will be justified.

There are debts to contemporaries which should also be acknowledged. Once again Robert Graves proved a provocative guide through this mythic terrain, particularly in his comments on the story of Odysseus in *The Greek Myths.* I should have been quite unable to follow Odysseus on his journey through the underworld without R. F. Paget's bold, pioneering work to uncover the Cumaean Oracle of the Dead, as recorded in his book *In the Footsteps of Orpheus* (The Scientific Book Club 1967), and without the further research into that important site reported by my friend Robert Temple in his *Netherworld* (Century 2002). For inspiration about the nature of the rituals on Aiaia, I drew on Normandi Ellis's translations from the Egyptian Book of the Dead in *Awakening Osiris (Phanes Press 1988),* and I found Peter Kingsley's illuminating study of Parmenides, *In the Dark Places of Wisdom* (Element Books 1999), to be an invaluable study of incubation rituals (as well as of so much else) in the Velian culture of Hellenic Italy. I strongly recommend all these books to those who wish to know more about the oracular and initiatory rites that lie behind this work of fiction.

Then there are other friends to thank: Sarah Tregellas, who sent me photographs of Ithaca, an island I hope to visit one day; Keith Sagar who generously shared his thoughts on the *Odyssey;* Jules Cashford who nurtured my faith in this enterprise, and John Moat whose wise good humour focussed my imagination. The encouragement of my editors Jane Johnson and Emma Coode was there for me throughout, as was, indispensably, the patient help of my wife Phoebe Clare.

L.C.
The Bell House
2004